PARADISE
OF DEATH

Also by Frank Orenstein:

The Man in the Gray Flannel Shroud
Murder on Madison Avenue
A Candidate for Murder

PARADISE OF DEATH

An Ev Franklin Mystery

Frank Orenstein

ST. MARTIN'S PRESS
NEW YORK

Library of Congress Cataloging-in-Publication Data

Orenstein, Frank.
    Paradise of death.

    "A Thomas Dunne book."
    I. Title.
PS3565.R39P37   1988   813'.54   87-28680
ISBN 0-312-01486-4

First Edition

10 9 8 7 6 5 4 3 2 1

For Chuck and Ilse
Companions on the long lurch
down Madison Avenue

There is something extremely pleasant, and even touching . . . in this peculiarity of needlework, distinguishing women from men . . . . The slender thread of silk or cotton [carries] off what would otherwise be a dangerous accumulation of morbid sensibility.

—Nathaniel Hawthorne,
The Marble Faun

Nat, baby, you don't know the half of it.
—Ev Franklin

PARADISE
OF DEATH

❑
ONE
❑

The island of San Sebo was a tropical paradise; all the travel agents said so, so it must have been true. As is often the case with a tropical paradise, however, life teemed and crowded in on itself. The Seboans reproduced until they overwhelmed the resources and were forced to live on a subsistence level. The jungle pushed in and new growth crowded out the old. As life was created it consumed the older, tired forms of existence, and the world was as relentless as it was beautiful.

The vulture and the barracuda and the crab were the island garbagemen. What man threw out the vulture tore apart, unless it landed in the water; in that case the barracuda and the crab took over, with help from the occasional shark. Lesser forms of life consumed most of what remained. And after that the sun rotted what little was left and returned it to the soil. In good times the scavengers got pig and poultry, but once in a while, when they were particularly lucky, they got tourist. This was generally not mentioned in the travel brochures. Tourist was a special treat, even though, if a cavil is permitted, it frequently runs to fat. On the other hand, since San Sebo was for the very rich, sometimes it wasn't all that fatty, being too eaten out by malice to put on weight, despite the elegance of its diet. Lucky was the scavenger who got himself a rich, malicious tourist. Lucky the crab; lucky the vulture; lucky, lucky, the barracuda and the shark.

Jane and I were there for the annual meeting of the board of Finch, Rowan, & Hyde, the ad agency we both worked for, I as the research director and Jane as my assistant. One of the dividends of our being married was that we could be put in the same room—in this case the same bungalow—when we traveled for the agency, which meant that it cost them only a pittance more to have both of us there slaving for the greater glory of Finch, Rowan, & Hyde. Ed Jorgensen, the company president, was never loath to get something for next to nothing, especially when he could point out when it was time to talk about raises that we really should take into account the fact that he had sent us to San Sebo, which, he would emphasize, was something Mr. and Mrs. Everett Franklin would otherwise scarcely be able to afford "unless"—laugh, laugh— "you've been ripping off the company."

When we were shown to the bungalow assigned to us, one of the back ones without a view of the Caribbean, we found a squashed mango on the steps. It had fallen from the tree in front, and judging by its condition, it had fallen some days ago. It lay there half squashed and half decayed, the lush scent of the fruit competing with the equally sweet stink of the rotting flesh; the air was full to the point of trembling with both odors, corruption and perfume, life and death, the future and the past.

Nobody ever showed up to sweep the fruit away, and Jane and I were too annoyed to do it ourselves, preferring to let it

2

remain as a source of pleasurable irritation, a little like a cavity in a back tooth that the tongue keeps seeking out in spite of the pain. And that mango was the perfect symbol, in a way, for San Sebo itself and for everything that happened there. San Sebo, part heaven and part hell. San Sebo, a paradise, a paradise of death.

TWO

Finch, Rowan, & Hyde is either the seventh or tenth largest ad agency on Madison Avenue, depending on what accounts we've gained or lost most recently. I say that not boastfully, though some of my efforts have contributed to Finch, etc.'s, ascendancy. For instance, there was our recent discovery that 14 percent of female heads of households chose for the family breakfast cereal whatever it might be that would best shut the kiddies up at table so that mommy could get on with her own affairs, whether nursing a hangover or anything else, even if it meant larding the cereal with enough sugar to enrich every dentist within a twenty-mile radius. Following that, the television campaign featured breakfast scenes with the family softly swilling in a state of catatonic bliss. The client's brand took off like a rocket.

And I speak not sadly, even though both Jane and I would much prefer to be living on the apple orchard we bought about ninety miles north of the city in the Hudson Valley.

Instead, I remain defiant, despite the rash of articles in the weekly newspapers generally available at the checkout counters in supermarkets; articles that state more or less bluntly that any association with Finch, etc., is likely to subject the associator to the same kind of curse that was whammied onto the hapless crew that gathered around during the opening of King Tut's tomb a couple of generations ago.

Nothing is going to happen to me or to Jane or to anyone else, and this is the story about what happened and what's going to not happen from now on.

It all began with that damned meeting of the board on San Sebo. To begin telling it requires a brief discussion of that dizzy American institution, the board of directors of the modern major corporation. In the first place, nobody really knows how people get to be members of the board, except for the one or two who are executives of the corporation or former executives thereof. The rest are members of the board because they're already members of the board and are up for reelection, a meaningless formality with a foregone conclusion.

Second, if there is one thing members of boards do better than anybody else in the world, it's fall asleep at meetings. Theoretically, they set policy for the coming year, but with few modifications, the meetings simply endorse policies already proposed by the corporate staff. There's one exception to this general rule; they're mostly all pretty much on the ball when the agenda gets around to discussing the location for the next meeting. Should it be Bermuda, Sea Island, Pebble Beach (Marvelous golfing at Pebble Beach!), or Maui?

Then, when it's time to talk about the reports from the Comptroller or the Director of Property Acquisitions or the Vice President for Legal Affairs and Taxes, it's off like a shot to dreamland once again.

A reasonable supposition, however, is that at the conclusion of the meeting, to a man the board will bolt from the

5

tomb of the board room and dive into the private dining salon for cocktails and swell eats prior to seeking whatever diversions the thoughtfully chosen locale might offer. Only this time, there on San Sebo, one of the kids remained asleep, slumbering serenely, it may be hoped, though not presumed, in the arms of the Lord forever.

The morning had begun with an informal snack of coffee and sweet rolls in the anteroom outside the meeting room itself. I got there about 8:30 to make sure the place was in proper order. (It wasn't; it never is. It was set up for an audience with a single speaker up front, instead of for a gathering of equals around a long table. An outsize crossing of bellmen's palms with silver soon corrected the situation, which I suspect is built into the system so that the various hotel staffs can be properly compensated for the inconvenient necessity of having guests on the premises. Hilton, Sheraton, Hyatt, Marriott et al., please take note.)

There even ahead of me was Ed Jorgensen, in his dual role as president of Finch, Rowan, & Hyde and chairman of the board. With his customary warmth he observed, "Oh. It's you, Franklin. Beginning to wonder if you were here. There may be trouble, damn it."

To show there were no flies on me, I said casually, "Yeah, I know all about it, Ed. Olds and Holland, right?" Olds and Holland were two board members I had heard the night before were headed for some kind of showdown.

"Olds and Holland, wrong," Ed replied testily. "Don't mix these things up, damn it! We've got enough trouble. It's Olds and Lamoureux," he snapped, naming still another member of the elect.

I held my tongue. Maybe there was trouble with Olds and Lamoureux, but there was trouble with Olds and Holland as well, though if Big Ed Jorgensen didn't know about it, I wasn't going to be the one to spring the surprise. "Oh," I said. "My mistake. What's up? Lamoureux got the hots for Lizzie Olds? Something like that?" Madam Olds was such that if anyone had dared to gaze at her seventy years of righteous indignation without glancing indirectly through a mirror, I'd estimate an uncomfortable likelihood he'd be turned to stone.

"Damn it, cut that kind of talk! You never know who's going to walk in." Ed was nervous, it would be safe to conclude. "No, the problem is that George Lamoureux's bank has some shaky farm loans outstanding, farmers going bust, that kind of thing. And the Olds Media Group is his biggest depositor. And—"

"—and Henry Olds is threatening to close out his account, I bet."

"That's it. It's nothing to do with us. Nothing to do with Finch, Rowan, & Hyde, but I've got a feeling we could get caught in the crossfire if we don't watch our step. So for God's sake, be careful!"

"Trust me, Ed," I said, pouring myself a cup of coffee and grabbing a sweet roll.

Over the next few minutes the board members and their wives made their several entrances. It was tradition for the wives to show up for that first informal breakfast so that they could greet each other, make plans for the day and the evening, and, all too often, decide whom to dislike the most. First to arrive was Dorothy Braun, dean of a Midwest college that had a high-powered marketing department specializing in advertising. She gave class to the proceedings, disliked nobody, was disliked by nobody—for a wonder—and despite an irrelevant and possibly nervous tic that caused her to break out in occasional speeches about truth in advertising and the necessity thereof, was a good kid to have on the premises.

Jane came in at almost the same moment and with obvious relief took Ms. Braun in tow for a chat. It was Jane's function at these wakes to be pleasant and helpful to the women in attendance, and Dorothy Braun was the only one she could be certain wouldn't embark on a wail of desperation about how terrible the price of Beluga caviar with powdered blue-white diamond sauce was getting to be.

That was one down and many more to go. The Oldses were

next, Henry and Elizabeth. Henry, well over seventy, was remarkably well preserved, like a fossilized stick of wood: dry, spare, and harder than iron. He boasted a permanent sardonic grin, and owned the only set of false tusks I have ever seen that appeared to have been specially crafted in dragon yellow. On the other hand, maybe they were real; they looked chillingly authentic.

Elizabeth looked like—well, she had prior rights, so the liner must have been named after her. She sailed in rather than entered, a magnificent prow cleaving the ocean of air in front of her, her inevitable rope of pearls standing nearly horizontal to the ground until cascading off the edge and plunging earthward to dangle freely, rather as I imagine a temporarily disengaged hangman's noose would dangle. She was famous for being the grimly indefatigable chairperson of every ladies' auxiliary her local pastor could invent. Good Works on behalf of her church were a driving force for Elizabeth Olds, though there were those who wondered whether she was bent on walking in the way of the Lord or whether she hoped that by setting a proper example she could lead Him into walking in the way of Elizabeth Olds. She was a good woman, in several of the worst meanings of the words.

Henry was talking as they came. "No substance to the man, no substance at all. Made of air he is, he and his company. What grandpa Biedermeier would have called a *luftmensch*."

"I know, my dear," his lady said, "and you're absolutely right not to even consider his offer."

"Oh, I didn't say that, Lizzie. Not at all. He comes up with the right figure, it's no skin off my banana where he gets the money, is it?"

"Henry Olds, don't you dare!" Her voice went up an octave, which put her just about in the basso profundo range, and she looked at her husband, whose yellows were bared in a grin, then collected herself as she realized the peasantry was at hand. She stopped and extended a hand toward Ed Jorgensen. "How nice to see you again, Mr. Jorgensen," she exclaimed in tones of heartfelt insincerity. "We both look forward so to these meetings."

8

Henry cackled. "Yeah, gives me a chance to catch up on my sleep. Which reminds me. Anything to put in that coffee, cut the caffeine?" He winked like an ancient satyr. "How about it, young fellow," he said to me, "think you can rustle up a touch of cognac?"

Mrs. O looked irritated, but held her tongue, which must have been a weighty burden. A bar was set up in the corner for the pre-luncheon cocktail session. I found a bottle of Remy Martin nestling there, and handed it into Henry Olds's bony mitt. He splashed a dollop into the cup the attendant had filled with coffee for him, considered it with pursed lips, and then added some more.

Mrs. Olds was ominously near to the thunderbolt-hurling mode, but fortunately the rest of the party poured in en masse, and the room was atremble with shrill greetings and more false warmth than a forced air heating system might reasonably be expected to provide. The Lamoureuxs, who Ed Jorgensen had expected might start trouble with Henry Olds, headed directly for the Oldses, and contrary to expectation, Dolly Lamoureux cried with delight, real or assumed, at the sight of the other couple. "Henry!" she exclaimed. "Elizabeth! How good to see you. Isn't it, dear?" she added to her husband George, who had the good grace to hang back several feet while in the presence of the man likely to force his bank into receivership.

"Yeah," George said.

Henry grinned, his teeth a shade yellower and a tad longer than a moment earlier. Elizabeth nodded courteously to the new arrivals, though managing to give the impression that she was laboring under the burden of a sprained neck.

A moment later, the Hollands, Randolph and Loretta, made their appearance. Randolph Holland was the only world-class figure on the board. He owned or controlled a major share of television stations, newspapers, radio stations, and magazines throughout the country, and in several foreign lands as well. He was a media monarch, and as such he was feared and worshipped, if there's a difference, by many people who would never have admitted it.

"Hiya, folks," he said. "How ya doin'?" Holland affected a man-of-the-people manner of speech, a manner he did not come by naturally. When he had first begun to assemble his media empire he was roundly snubbed as a Johnny-come-lately by those who regarded themselves as his superiors, and his way of rubbing salt in their wounds was to act as they expected him to act.

Loretta, Mrs. Holland, was a filly of a different color. One of Randolph's English acquisitions, she had been a cover girl some ten years previously, and was cooler and more elegant than royalty, and too tall, willowy, blonde, and flawless to be real. She looked about the room with a graciously noncommittal smile, nodding and stretching or retracting her lips according to the degree of acknowledgment due the party on whom her eye had landed.

Holland strode directly over to Henry Olds and clapped that brittle frame on the back. "Hiya, stud, how ya doin'?" he hooted. In concert, the gentleman so addressed bared his teeth, while, from her seat against the wall, his spouse compressed her mouth even more tightly, averaging out to an absolute zero of response for the two.

Such was typical Randolph Holland behavior. When he had first begun his empire, he had tried being pleasant and had found that his good behavior was regarded generally as toadyism. Both personal and corporate doors were shut against him. Then he had fallen seriously ill, and, as the saying goes, he had lingered at death's door for weeks until he realized that even that portal was not to be opened to admit him. Once he had absorbed this truth, together with the knowledge that life was not forever, his character and his tactics had changed. He became aggressive, even deliberately insulting, and as meanspirited in business matters as a Dickensian banker.

This led to almost immediate success, and the adjectives crude, ruthless, and vulgar, were overnight replaced by forthright, determined, and earthy. There was a lesson to be learned here, though not by Boy Scouts or aspiring saints.

While he was bellowing forth his unwelcome welcomes and bonhomie, Mrs. Holland suddenly brightened. "Ken," she exclaimed, "Ken Tillson! Darling!"

To my surprise, I saw our TV production chief, who had assured me only the night before that he had no intention of showing up to meet the board, stride into the room. Kenny was down on San Sebo to supervise the making of a series of television commercials, and to accommodate those members of the board and their spouses who might have some interest in watching the process.

"Darling!" Ken echoed, planting a kiss on the lady's cheek. "How are you, dear? It's so good!"

"Oh, it is, darling. It's been *so* long." Ken had told me he and Loretta Holland had known each other in their native London years earlier, when they were both getting started, and before, naturally, she had met Randolph Holland.

"Well, do let's huddle in a corner and have a little quack-quack gab-gab," Kenny said, "and we can tell each other all about it." Loretta tittered, which didn't fit her current image of the great lady, but which somehow seemed much more natural. The two of them retired to a sofa against the window wall and settled down for what, if I judged correctly from their expressions, was an eminently satisfying session of slandering and slicing such friends and acquaintances as they had in common. Both were apparent adepts at character assassination.

Meanwhile, Dolly Lamoureux had moved in closer on the Oldses, asserting her priority over Randolph Holland. "Do let me get you another cup of coffee, Henry," she crooned, "and would you like a tippytap more cognac to kill the caffeine? I'll bet you would!" She proceeded to oblige, and I learned by watching that a tippytap is somewhere between half and two-thirds of a cup. I also learned that Elizabeth Olds had muscles in her lips that enabled her to tighten them even when starting from a compressed position. I wondered vaguely if she had the talent to swallow her own head.

And so it went for half an hour. Ed Jorgensen darted about

the room jollying everyone up as best he could, and keeping George Lamoureux and Henry Olds apart. I stayed with Jane and Dorothy Braun as much as possible, though the latter's lectures on Morality, Advertising, Truth, and You, were a shade on the tedious side, particularly when I knew I'd be expected to cluck my shock at the end of every other verbal exclamation point.

Finally, the board was herded into the meeting room by Big Ed. As we filed in, with a kittenish wink ill-suited to her all too solid substance, Dolly Lamoureux slipped an alcoholic re-fill to Henry Olds. At the same time, Loretta Holland called to her husband that she needed some money in case she decided to trot down to the tax-free goodies outlets. Randolph went over to oblige, and from the position she assumed while accepting the cash I learned something more about the woman. She stood with her right arm partly extended in a V-shape, elbow down, palm up and adangle to be sullied by her husband's cash. Her head was turned away from the action as she continued to talk to Ken Tillson. It reminded me of a liquor study I had once done for the agency. We had asked dedicated bourbon drinkers to draw a picture of a man drinking something alien, like scotch, and a typical picture showed an arm in a V-shape, just as Loretta Holland's was now, and a hand barely holding a glass. But when we asked them to draw a picture of a man drinking bourbon, the arm and the glass and the mouth formed almost a perfect circle.

They were distancing themselves from the scotch in the first drawing, but expressing unity with the bourbon in the second. (To solve the problem we took ads in newspapers and regional magazines in the bourbon belt, showing scotch not as something that New York and San Francisco sophisticates consumed in penthouses, but as something bourbon drinkers could serve at the backyard barbecue or in the family room in front of the TV set. Sneaky, huh? But it worked.)

So this girl was distancing herself, in real life—no drawing—from the sordid lucre. Money, in Loretta Holland's opinion, took its grace from her, rather than the other way round. (Fat chance, I told myself.)

When we had assembled in the meeting room, I looked around. I didn't realize it then, but it was the last time each and every one of us would ever be together. If I had known it, maybe I could have arranged a group portrait, something suitable for framing, and even to serve as a model for the sculptors on Madame Tussaud's payroll.

The session commenced. Dorothy Braun, the board secretary, read the minutes of the last meeting. Henry Olds drained his cup and fell asleep. The treasurer being absent, Ed Jorgensen read his report for him. George Lamoureux fell asleep; I managed to keep my eyes open, but then I was only an employee and was supposed to deny myself the luxury of a nap. The formalities over, the first item on the agenda was charitable contributions to be made by Finch, etc. This is another singular aspect of the American board of directors; they realize they have to support something worthy, since their public relations firms have told them so. Consequently they follow two general rules: They give to genteel, non-controversial causes, and they give to causes their wives are interested in. That's how all those ballet companies, museums, symphonies, and parks associations do so well—the ladies are very cultured and, well, ladylike. Everybody stayed awake for this section, else they'd have been in the marital soup if their spouses' interests weren't properly funded.

We blathered on through my part, in which I told them of the outlook for the national economy and what that meant for the agency. (With the sinking dollar U.S. exports would be looking up, and we were planning on several campaigns abroad for our clients, working through our overseas offices or foreign affiliates.) My part finished, I was dismissed, after a few desultory questions from Dorothy Braun to show me that somebody listened, somebody cared.

The wives were still in the anteroom. Even Loretta Holland had foregone her trip to the shops and was behind the bar showing the barman how to mix drinks properly. Jane rolled her eyes at me in silent horror to let me know how much she had been suffering. Dolly Lamoureux was grouped with Loretta Holland at the bar, but they seemed to have little to say to each other. Elizabeth Olds was off by herself doing her lip-compression exercises, which may, for all I know, have had some aerobic and therefore healthful component. And she was knitting furiously, as if attacking her yarn with plastic daggers. The pointy end of the needles disgorged a partially completed pullover in selected colors of joylessness—mouse brown, dun yellow, and off battleship gray.

What the ladies all appeared to be doing mostly was waiting, waiting for the board's mid-morning break.

The moment came at approximately 11 o'clock. The boys all rushed for the men's room, except for Henry Olds. They had left him sleeping, a condition from which his wife relieved him by marching into the board room and braying. He came out, smiled blearily, and went over to the bar for a mid-morning cola. Loretta poured while the bartender looked annoyed. Dolly picked up a rum bottle and looked at the old boy, raising her eyebrows coyly. He grinned, she tipped the bottle. He took his drink back into the board room after a wink that took in all the ladies present. Anyway, almost all the women; maybe not his wife.

Elizabeth raised herself from her chair and went over to the bar. She ignored both the Holland and Lamoureux girls, declining even to look at them, and said to the bartender, "Let me have a cup of coffee. Some people have no sense at all." She took the cup, backed away as if from her mooring at a Hudson River pier, and after creaming and sugaring at the side table, chugged into the other room. "Henry, I want you to drink this coffee, and put down that—oh, for heaven's sake, you've damn near finished it, haven't you! Really, Henry, you should know better. That woman's just trying to butter you up, and sometimes I think you just don't have any common sense either. Now drink this, you hear?" I think she used a megaphone to make sure the offenders got the message.

The other board members straggled back in, took their coffee or soft drinks, chatted up the ladies, and then were called back to the meeting by Ed Jorgensen.

Another hour and a half went by before the meeting broke. Mrs. Olds continued knitting in the interim, again slaying the mythical beasts that lurked within her yarn. Dolly Lamoureux sat like a deflated balloon, all the bubbles drained out by her attempts to charm Henry Olds, and still in a state of doubt as to what she had accomplished. Loretta Holland looked too uninterested even for boredom.

Once again the boys rushed out and headed for the john, except for Henry Olds, who remained in his customary dreamland. Elizabeth sighed the sigh of the militant martyr, thereby rattling most of those present, as well as several windows, and went inside. "Henry," she said. Then, "Henry!" she shrieked. "My God, Henry!"

She came out and looked about, and for once her lips were parted. "He's dead," she said. "He's dead. You killed him, damn you," she went on, but it wasn't possible to know whom she was accusing. Possibly all of us, possibly the world. Or just possibly Dolly Lamoureux, who had been feeding the old boy all the booze she could get into him without a funnel.

"You did it, damn you," she said in a hoarse whisper that I knew somehow was audible as far away as Havana, borne on wings of fury. "But you're still finished, you and your George. It's mine, now, all of it, and you're out—you and your George and your damned bank."

She turned to Loretta Holland. "And you, you can stop it too, that uppity smile, looking down on the rest of us. It's mine, and it's going to stay mine." She clenched her fists. "I'd die before I let you get what's mine, do you hear!"

They heard.

Her voice rose, and she swayed slightly as she faced the room. "My Henry is dead, and you killed him." She choked out a sob, but tearlessly.

The room was still. A door opened. A dark-skinned man, his shiny cheeks darker than life under a white chef's hat, announced, "Ladies and gentlemen, luncheon is served."

At that very moment Randolph Holland strode in, back from the men's room, his fingers still straying to make sure his

I 5

zipper was closed. In typical style he said, "Good! If I don't get something to eat soon, I tell ya, I'm gonna drop dead!"

We were frozen in position. Only three sounds penetrated the spell: A bird screamed shrilly in the trees beyond the clearing; there was a protesting creak from a wicker chair as Elizabeth Olds's head struck it while descending to the floor; and the lady's pearls bounced a staccato escape across the tiles, at long last disencumbered of the rope that had emprisoned them to her neck and bosom.

❑
THREE
❑

It may get to be a little clearer, though not much, if I go back to the night before. At least that will explain something about the Hollands and the Oldses and about Henry Olds's probably platonic lambchop, Carlla the Swedish Bombshell. That was Friday, and Jane and I had arrived in the afternoon. We planned on leaving early on Sunday, after I had done my act at the board meeting and then had spent Saturday afternoon lazing on the beach.

Shortly after arrival I looked up Ken Tillson, down to supervise the creation of commercials for *Glo and Get It,* a hair toner account we had in the shop. (Yes, that's "toner," all right, "dye" not being classy enough these days.) "Hey, Kenny," I said, "let's have dinner tonight. Jane's down with me. Is Carla working with you?"

"Yeah, she's here. And it's C-A-R-DOUBLE-L-A these days."

"Huh?"

He shrugged. "Don't ask me. I think her astrologer said it's got better vibes that way." He lifted his eyebrows, which tilted his hairpiece forward so that he assumed his characteristic look of an English sheepdog peering through his rug. And as a matter of fact Ken Tillson had come over from London about twenty years ago to work in the States. He had all the affectations of the pseudo-artistic types who make TV commercials: the lifted eyebrows, the insistence on calling everybody, especially people he didn't like, daahling, the affected drawl, and above all, a hypertrophic gossip gland that was almost never turned off, probably not even at night.

"Anyway," he went on, "dear Carlla is with us. Natch. After all, it's a board meeting and old pussycat Olds will be here and looking for her."

"And if he didn't find her?"

"Listen, sweetheart, that question don't compute, like they say. With Olds sitting on the board, not to mention his sitting down hard on maybe five percent of Finch's stock, there is no way he couldn't find her. Not until I decide I need a change of jobs. No, sir, duckie, no way."

I loved to listen to Kenny's voice when he was dispensing dirt. It took on a deliciously thin quality, somewhere between a 1930's phonograph record, a lovelorn duck, George Bush digging his way out of a hole (again), or any two out of three, depending on where your political sympathies lie.

"What's with Carlla and the old boy, anyway? I mean, his wife comes down to these meetings, doesn't she? And it's a pretty damn small island, no?"

"Oh, come on. Nothing goes on. He's like a hundred and eight, I'll bet, and he just likes to look. I'd say the wife figures it keeps him out of worse trouble, having him where she can have an eye on him at least."

"Well, that's not our problem, I hope. Anyway, bring Carlla along. Meet in the bar about seven, okay?"

"Right you are, sweetheart. Looking forward."

When Jane and I got to the bar we spotted Ken hiding behind an enormous concoction in a brandy snifter, senior size, pineapple stick jutting out, orange wedge skewered on the edge, cherry stem curling over, and shining through it all the bright varnish tone of the local rum, a variety that never made it to the mainland, but only for good and sufficient reason. Carlla was sitting next to him drinking something pinkish; it looked like liquefied bubble gum on the rocks, the kind of non-alcoholic horror a top model would consume to protect her highly visible physical assets from premature deterioration.

We exchanged hellos, and Jane and I drew up chairs and ordered drinks, a scotch for her—one ice cube and a little water—and a vodka martini on the rocks for me, which here in rum country made me into a late twentieth-century American version of an early nineteenth-century Englishman sipping his hot tea in some unlikely outpost of Empire.

I looked at Carlla fondly. "It's good to see you, Carlla. I hear your astrologer has been working on your name."

She looked at me cynically. "Don't believe everything you hear. Especially from this one," she added, jerking her head toward Ken Tillson. "I just hit twenty-eight, the age nobody believes, and any little gimmick to gloss up the image—well, modeling doesn't go on forever, you know."

"You've got nothing to worry about," Jane said, "not with that face."

"And figure," I added.

It was true. Ken had told me that Carlla, formerly Carla, even more formerly Helga Swenson, was the product of a northern Minnesota farm of second generation Swedes, and she looked it. Ash blonde, nearly six feet tall, cornflower eyes, and a bust that would have made Mae West look like a sheet of plywood. Carlla was a big blonde, a dumb big blonde; but that didn't mean what you might think it meant. Carlla was a professional dumb big blonde. To put it another way, Carlla was a smart dumb big blonde who knew how to play the act for all that it was worth. Nobody's patsy, she. Au contraire.

"Look," Jane said, "I know a girl in your position has problems, but doesn't it worry you to have Henry Olds snuffling around when his wife is just down the hall? I mean, well, you know."

"Oh, come on," Carlla returned, "nothing much goes on, and his wife is just as happy knowing where he is. You think I'd be on this *Glo and Get It* campaign if Oldsie wasn't on your board and a big stockholder on top of that?"

"Sure you would, darling," Ken Tillson said, reaching over to pat the big and not so dumb blonde on the hand, "sure you would. I'd insist on it."

"Yeah, I bet. Anyway, let's skip it. The old boy likes me and I like him, and if it ever got physical it'd only be a wrestling match to see which one of us gets to sit on the other's lap." She laughed. "And he'd end up on mine. I got the weight on him. Why don't we get something to eat? I'm tired of sitting around here discussing my no-sex life."

San Sebo being somewhat less endowed with restaurants than the island of Manhattan, we ended up across the veranda in a room that matched the bar right down to the imitation thatching on the pseudo Mayan, or maybe African, roof that covered it, supported by poles that looked every bit as if they had been hewn out of coconut palms, despite my uneasy certainty that there had to be a made-in-Japan logo loitering at the base of each.

We talked about the meetings that were to start in the morning. "Jane and I are here for the morning session," I said, "and I guess we'll put the afternoon in on the beach, after the luncheon. Then on Sunday we check out, thank God, and get away from these people. How about you two?"

"Oh, I don't know," Ken said, "two days, maybe three. Maybe even four. Depends on whether that board of yours and their wives come around and want guided tours of the wonderful world of television commercial production. I don't care, really, so long as I don't have to go to your meetings."

Jane asked, "If they keep coming around, doesn't that get the costs way up? I mean if they add to the production time?"

Ken looked disgusted. "Sweetheart," he said, "where've

you been the last ten years? Nobody cares how much this one costs. Not Finch, and not Rowan or Hyde either, wherever and whoever they may be."

"They don't?" I asked. "You're a lucky pussycat, Tillson. I go over budget and I get an accountant's toothmarks on my throat."

"This is different, dummy dear," Ken explained. "You've heard of the Internal Revenue Service, right? Well, those boys don't always take too kindly to trips to tropical islands when somebody claims them as a business deduction. But the board of an advertising agency, they've got to know how commercials are made, right? Right! So they've *got* to come to this rotten old desert island, even when they hate it, and look, you IRS mothers, you ought to give us double deductions for hardship and dengue fever and jungle rot and such like, right? Right! JEEEZUS! The ways the rich can figure out to get richer." He shook his head.

"You two kids ought to stick around," Carlla said to Jane and me. "There's going to be fireworks around here, I bet you."

"It's no fun for us here," Jane explained. "I get to be a lady's maid, sort of, and Ev's a kind of office boy. We're getting out, soon as we can. Anyway, what kind of fireworks?"

Carlla frowned. "Well, I shouldn't talk so damned much, but you know Oldsie, he's not a bad guy, really, but I guess the only thing he's got left is how he can make people dance when he says they should dance."

"Yeah," Ken said, "that plus ten million bucks."

Carlla ignored him. "Well, this super big shot on your board, the one who owns newspapers and TV stations all over the place, you know?"

"Randolph Holland?" I asked.

"That's the one. He's trying to buy out the Olds people. Henry told me all about it and how he's stringing this Holland character along and has no intention of selling out. He just wants big shot Holland to kiss ass for a while and then get nothing out of it but a great big bunch of thanks."

"I don't get it," Jane said. "Holland's got newspapers,

magazines, TV stations, and God knows what, all over the country. Olds has got the same thing, but in miniature. In one state. Hell, maybe only in one city."

Carlla gave us a knowing smile, teeth gleaming, eyes sparkling, head thrown back to show us the swanlike neck and the glistening highlights in the hair. It was blinding. "Ah, yes. I'm glad you mentioned that. Henry told me all about it. He likes to tell me about it. It's like sex for the old dear these days. The Oldses made their money like a million years ago, before taxes, before laws about what you could own, what you could do, how you could do it. So they don't just own the paper and the TV and radio stations; they've got everything else around too—the meat packing plant, the big department store, and I guess the mayor and the chief of police as well. Henry talks about the Olds Foundation hospital, the Olds auditorium— and you know what? There's even parking places all over this dumb town that have Private Parking signs on them, and they're just for him and his old lady. They haven't got any kids," she added.

"Anyway," she went on, "Henry says that the Randolph people are overextended. They need cash, and Henry's little kingdom is loaded; he runs it just for him and madam. He doesn't do any branching out anymore—too old, I guess— and he leaves the money in, instead of taking it out and paying taxes. Meantime, he and the wife are like king and queen of the whole town, and they like it that way. So your Mr. Holland thinks he's going to buy out my Mr. Olds with his junk bonds and big promises, but he sure ain't. No leveraged buy-outs for Henry Olds. He'll just let Holland dangle for a while and then tell him that."

"Carlla, doll," I said. "Can I ask you a personal question, sort of?" She nodded. "How did you learn about leveraged buy-outs?" I asked.

"I took it in with my mother's milk," she answered. "In this game a girl can't know too much."

"That's rotten," Kenny said. "I don't give a hoot about Randolph, but his wife Loretta is an old chum of mine. We met back in the old country, in London. She used to be a

22

model, too, just like you, sweetie, and we hit it off, the two of us."

I shook my head in admiration. "Ken," I said, "you know more people than anybody I've ever met." It was true; Ken Tillson contracted friendships like other people contract diseases, indiscriminately and with infinite ease.

He laughed. "Oh, Loretta Holland—Loretta Saunders in those days—came from the same kind of people I did, the great overwashed and underchic middle class, before she got to be high society. I'd go over to her place—she lived with her folks—for dinner once in a while. You know the kind of household: Dinner was whatever Ma thought it was time to clear out of the icebox, and she did it with a cigarette dangling out of the middle of her mouth with an ash on it about two inches long. Nice people. Relaxed. And so was Loretta in those days. I hope your Oldsie doesn't screw things up for her."

Carlla looked indifferent. "He will if he can, Kenny. He will if he can." She yawned. "Oldsie's got something rotten in store for everybody. A regular old Santa Claus, is what. He's going to string along Holland some more, but let his wife think maybe he'll finally sell out. She'll just about poop at that idea. Nobody ever heard of the old broad any place it matters, but back in Nowheresville she's top dog, and I do mean dog, and that she wants to hold on to. Then she knows about me, natch, and she ought to know she's got nothing to worry about there, but I wouldn't put it past the old boy to jab the needle in and let her get the idea she's going to be traded in on a new model. Namely me. So she'll poop some more."

"I'll bring a broom," Jane said.

"Better make it a whole truck," Carlla said. "Lizzie Olds is a big one. Besides, Henry's got it in for somebody else on the board, just like he's doing with Holland."

"Who?" I asked. "For God's sake, *who?*" My voice went up. I must have sounded like an owl.

But Carlla was bored. "Oh, I don't know. I didn't listen after a while. It gets dull, you know? For me, anyway, even if

2 3

it does send Henry to the moon, just talking about it." She looked at her watch, and the watch looked back at her like the gift it was from Henry Olds, diamond by diamond. "Listen, I've got to take a walk around and then get some sleep if I'm going to look right for tomorrow. And Kenny, don't expect me to be using this *Glo and Get It* on camera. I got a friend tried it and she ended up like a twenty-five-year-old poodle with mange." She stood. "Let's go."

The rest of us stood too. Jane put out her hand. "Hold on a sec," she said. "Carlla, honey, I get the idea if someone asks you to put on a pair of black stockings with a rosebud garter, plus a tight black corset, and carry a whip, you wouldn't give it a second thought."

Carlla frowned briefly. "Why not? If it makes someone happy. And if there's a little something in it for me. Why not?" she asked again, and looked at her watch for the answer. "Let's go," she repeated.

And that's how I got to find out about Olds and Holland before Ed Jorgensen did.

❑

FOUR

❑

The island nation of San Sebo is one of the actors in this comedy, and right here, with Henry Olds gradually growing cold and stiff in the board room of the San Sebo Grand Hotel, might be as good a spot as any to put in a few words about the place. Of course, Henry Olds, given the climate, might be growing more stiff than cold, but nevertheless, after the shock of his sudden demise, a rest period is in order.

King Manuel the Fortunate of Portugal dispatched one of his best explorers, Senhor Pedro Alvarez Cabral, in a westerly direction sometime in the year 1500. Ultimately, Cabral stepped ashore in Brazil, and that tended to overshadow his intermediate landing at a small island just to the east of Barbados, where he arrived after an inadvertent detour, otherwise known as a hurricane. Cabral uttered the ritual words that claimed the island for Christendom and the treasury of

King Manuel, and then left for greater prizes. This was one of the times that Manuel wasn't so fortunate.

Eventually, the Portuguese named the place São Sebastião, and stocked it with sugar plantations and African slaves. The slaves, who were, due to a massive lack of interest on the part of anybody else, now the natives, weren't up to coping with the nasalities of the Portuguese tongue; they called the place San Sebo.

In due course, the Spanish relieved the original discoverers of their uninteresting burden, accomplishing this by no more than a single shot at the governor's mansion, a wooden hut with a roof of palm fronds. The shot missed, but the Portuguese residents, all eight of them, were just as happy to be leaving, either for home or for the richer pickings of Brazil.

The Spanish, with the same morbid passion for tortured martyrs as their neighbors on the Iberian peninsula, maintained the island's name, simply adapting it to their own tongue. It was now San Sebastian. The natives continued to call it San Sebo.

The French were next, arriving in the late seventeenth century under the banner of the Sun King, Louis XIV. Even then, the national paranoia for contemplating all other languages as vicious and deliberate attacks by anti-monarchists on the perfection of their own was rampant in France, and led the conquerors to change the name completely. It was now Belle Isle. The natives, growing hungrier and ever more dispirited as the sugar plantations played out, scarcely noticed, and went on referring to their homeland as San Sebo.

Ownership shifted once again in the eighteenth century, during the glorious expansion of the British Empire. The English, always more secure about their own language than the French, generally regarded other tongues as imperfect attempts on the part of children or mental defectives to communicate in English. Since the island was more or less bow-shaped, two perky wings joined by a narrow band of land fronting on a lagoon and harbor of sorts, they concluded the natives were unsuccessfully trying to say that the insignificant spot in the ocean was called Saucybow. They kept the name.

The natives continued their misunderstanding that the name was San Sebo.

Nearly two centuries later, the British were in fiscal and military retreat, and the island was granted its independence. It was now the republic of San Sebo, just the way the natives had always known it was. To support itself, several sources of income were developed. London was blackmailed into providing conscience money for what was called the centuries of repression and slavery. The United States was blackmailed into sending funds on a regular basis to ensure equally regular denunciations of Cuban Communism. A medical school of no small merit was established to accommodate Americans who failed to gain entry into schools in their homeland. And above all, tourism was developed. Reinforced concrete hotels with balconies, casinos, gift shops, and guaranteed gourmet dining salons were crowded around the harbor, and private colonies for the unbelievably wealthy were created in the hills to either side of the harbor town.

One other event transpired to legitimize San Sebo's place in the comity of nations. A sixteenth-century Seboan named Sebo was discovered by local historians. This Sebo was distinguished by two achievements. First, he was visited in a dream by the Virgin Mary, who assured him that there was more than a touch of the old tar brush in the Holy Family, descended as they were from Sheba and Solomon. And second, he achieved instant sainthood for himself, moreover without benefit of clergy, and subsequently bestowed his name upon the island.

At one point, in an effort to bestir the Seboans into a fervor of patriotism, the government let it be known that the Vatican had marshalled its troops to combat this usurpation of their authority to decide who would or would not make sainthood. The local troops, all seventy-five of them, were likewise marshalled and the Vatican was declared defeated. Taxes were raised to pay for this highly necessary military adventure.

One last minor invasion brings the history of San Sebo up to date. An American patrol boat, wandering off course on its passage from San Juan to the Canal Zone, was approached by the Seboan police in a vessel approximately as threatening as a Papuan war canoe. The captain of the American boat, a devoted and nervous follower of a retired Pentagon lieutenant general whose views were so far to the right that it was rumored that even his stercoraceous effluvia were lily-white, fired a warning shot. It missed the patrol boat but struck and destroyed several Seboan huts and killed their occupants.

Reparations were paid, the chief of the Seboan police assumed command of all San Sebo on a permanent basis and established a mildly despotic regime. He was known as Sarge, and he figures importantly in this story. His word and his wishes were law, but he exacted only a modest levy on whatever little wealth the island produced. For instance, for each Seboan killed by the American gunfire the sum of $5,000 was paid, and Sarge assigned himself a modest ten percent. He called it a finder's fee, which was a phrase he had picked up from a Miami newspaper a tourist had left behind. (All written materials brought into the island were saved for Sarge's scrutiny; he had heard that the better class of dictatorship did things this way.)

So much for the history of San Sebo.

When the board meeting broke up so unceremoniously, we all professed to being unable to think of food, though of course after the long morning it was what most of us could think about best, except for the unprogrammed demise of Henry Olds, whose remains had been removed to the local morgue. Mrs. Olds was escorted to her room by Jane, the only one of the ladies with whom she was on speaking terms, and we went to lunch. So, we discovered, had all the other members of the party, though they sat at various tables around the dining room rather than gather together at the special board luncheon. It seemed more decent.

Ed Jorgensen asked us to join him at table. "Hell of a mess, isn't it," he said. "How is she? Still yelling bloody murder?"

"What can I say?" Jane replied. "I got her to bed with the

help of a doctor the hotel sent up. She had some pills on the dresser, Nembutal, and we gave her one to put her to sleep. But, yes, she's still yelling bloody murder. She says the Lamoureux woman killed Henry; then she says Mrs. Holland did it. And then she looks at me and the doctor and says we all hated him, we all did it, or 'they' did it—whoever they are." She pushed out a sigh. "She's hysterical, and it's very unpleasant, and listen, Ed, I didn't sign on for this kind of thing. I'm glad to have helped, but you're not going to dump it on me. It's not my problem."

"I know, I know, Jane. We'll get help. I appreciate your helping out. It's—it's—" He groped for the words.

"A pain in the ass?" I suggested.

"Right. A pain in the ass. Let's eat."

On these lesser Caribbean islands, the smart money bets on the local seafood, which tends to be fresh, while the beef, veal, and pork are as fatty and old as the chicken is stringy and old. We munched our way through our several selections, appetites stimulated rather than subdued by the occasion. What a tribute to the late Mr. Olds. I could visualize the obituary: "Grief-stricken by his sudden demise, everybody had swell eats, and in substantial quantity."

As we were finishing, the hotel manager approached the table. "Mr. Jorgensen," he said, "I'm sorry to trouble you, but Sarge requests you visit his offices in Government House when you have finished your lunch." He spoke in hushed tones, the only one to do so. But then he hadn't known Henry Olds as well as the rest of us.

"Who is Sarge, and why does he want to see me?" Ed asked. "And where is Government House?"

"Sarge is our chief of police," the manager explained. "I can only guess it concerns this, ah, unfortunate incident. And Government House," he concluded, looking embarrassed, "is on the second landing of the hotel. Just above the lobby level."

"Mm," Ed grunted, "about half an hour then. Ev, I want you with me." Jane looked ready to say she wasn't going to let me go. "Now, Jane, this isn't going to amount to a thing.

2 9

I'm sure it's going to be nothing more than formal Seboan regrets and seventeen papers to fill out. You know how these little places are about pomp and circumstance. And if Ev is with me, it'll look like more of a proper delegation. Got to keep these people happy," my sneaky, lying boss said to my wife.

Jane looked doubtful. "Okay, but I'm telling you, Ed Jorgensen, that I don't want you landing my husband in the seafood chowder again. There's been too much of that already."

It was a sweet and considerate concern that Jane expressed, but in this life we don't always get what we want, do we.

FIVE

We were ushered into Government House, an office on the second floor of the hotel clearly labelled Government House, by a policeman wearing khaki trousers, rubber shower sandals, and a T-shirt suggesting WHEN YOU NEED IT BAD— FLORIDA! A grossly overweight man of perhaps 275 pounds of flab draped in furls and swags across his six foot frame rose from behind a metal desk to greet us. His T-shirt, which read SARGE, rode up over a protuberance that served him handsomely as a stomach. The focal point of his being was a slit of a belly button that leered through the folds of fat like a one-eyed Mandarin contemplating nameless villainies.

However, he smiled brilliantly. "Gentlemen," he said, "please do have a seat." His accent was more nearly English than that of the other locals, and his choice of words was authentic mock-English gentleman. He snapped his fingers and the policeman hurriedly drew up two rattan chairs which I suspected had been lifted from the hotel lounge moments before our arrival. We sat.

"One of you gentlemen is Mr. Edward Jorgensen?" Sarge asked, his eyes shifting appraisingly from Ed to me and then back to Ed.

Ed nodded. "That's me."

"Good. I am very pleased to meet you. I asked you here because you are, I believe, in charge of the party where the"—his hand went from side to side as he groped for a delicate word—"unfortunate incident occurred. And the other gentleman?" The calculating eyes shifted to me.

"Ev Franklin," I said. "Mr. Jorgensen's, uh, aide." I don't know why I said 'aide'; something military about the situation elicited the response.

Sarge inclined his head ever so slightly. "Mr. Franklin," he said courteously. "May I offer you gentlemen a coffee? Something to drink, perhaps?"

Ed spoke for us both. "Thank you, no. We're both anxious to get back to our group." Translation: What are we doing here?

"Of course. I'll be brief. Put as plainly as possible, the body of the unfortunate Mr. Olds is now in hospital, where an autopsy will be performed. You know that San Sebo has a medical facility equal to any in the world. London, New York, any in the world." The grand sweep of his hand indicated the galactic excellence of this Seboan institution.

"We recognize that, Sarge," Ed said, not about to disagree at this point, at least until we found out what the man was after. "I know that will be a great comfort to Mrs. Olds. But is there anything we need to discuss?"

"Only that we will require your party to remain on the island until the autopsy is complete and we have the results. That should be no later than tomorrow morning or perhaps the afternoon. I trust no one will be inconvenienced?"

"Oh, I'm not sure," Ed protested. "Conceivably someone may have to call back to the States, but I shouldn't think that'd be any problem."

The urbanity was getting too thick to breathe through. It ended here, however.

"That," Sarge said firmly, "will not be possible, I'm sorry to say. The phones are out." He smiled ruefully. "I'm afraid the British Government has been late again—they're increasingly late, you know—with their reparations payments, and these were slotted for the overhaul of the phone system."

I spoke up. "No problem. Any of our people want to they can radio."

He shook his head sadly. "Unfortunately, no. The military are limiting access to radio communications for reasons of national security. Purely temporary, I'm sure."

Ed sighed with exasperation; he was unaccustomed to being overruled. "Now, Mr.—now Sarge, why don't we get down to cases. What is it exactly you're after? What are you trying to tell us? Let's have it straight."

"Very well. That suits me perfectly. What I'm saying is that your Mrs. Olds is screaming bloody murder over what I'm sure will turn out simply to be the death by natural causes of a very elderly gentleman whose time had come. On this island, with our diet and our poverty, he would have been long since in his grave. Good. If our autopsy shows that he was indeed murdered, then so be it. Let the truth prevail. This is a democracy, and the truth must out, eh, gentlemen?" He smiled benevolently.

"But," he added, pointing a finger at Ed Jorgensen the way nobody back home ever gets to point a finger at Ed Jorgensen except for Mrs. Ed, "if she is wrong, and I'm sure she is, then we cannot allow the lady to broadcast irresponsible accusations."

"Why not?" I asked. "Everybody will know the truth. What harm can she possibly do?"

"Harm enough." Sarge stood and went to a shabby, yellow-spotted map on the wall. He picked up a pointer and began a comic-opera military briefing. "Here, this tiny spot on the map is my country. San Sebo." He tapped the tiny spot, thus proving the point. "And here," he said, describing a large circle on the map, "is your country, Vast. Vast and rich."

3 3

He turned to face us, legs stiffly apart like a ten-cent General Patton, pointer horizontally held in both hands, stomach riding defiantly above. "One vast and rich, one small and poor. One dependent on tourism from the other. One hysterical female, one thoughtless, selfish, stupid female screams to your government and your press that her husband was murdered, and what happens to our most important source of income? Ruined. We are a proud people, gentlemen, and a silly woman like this can reduce us to begging, which we would never do. We will not live on charity!" he intoned, and I wondered whether the British and American taxpayers would be as delighted as I was to hear that. Of course, it wasn't charity the island was living on, but blackmail, if anyone wanted to tickle the niceties.

Ed clucked in some exasperation. "How long will all this take? We all have urgent business back home, and I know Mrs. Olds will want her husband's body taken back as well. Mr. Olds was a prominent citizen in his part of the country, you understand."

Ed made his last statement sound like a threat without it actually being one, which is a talent that goes along with being a top executive, but Sarge wasn't buying. "We on San Sebo," he said, nodding to indicate his appreciation of Henry Olds's eminence, "are delighted to have had his presence, no matter how briefly." He grinned, charmed by his own wit. "Nevertheless, we will follow the prescribed procedures. But be of good cheer, my friends. Enjoy this beautiful island. Fishing, golf, shopping, whatever you fancy. The hospital tells me the autopsy will almost certainly be completed tomorrow anyway, and you will be free to leave any time after that. And the dear lady will be able to take her husband, should she desire to remove him from our little paradise." The smile grew broader.

Another part of being a top executive is to know when you've had it. Ed stood. "Thank you. We'll be waiting. Meantime we'll take your advice and sample the local hospitality. And," he added, the shade of a thin edge to his voice, "we'll

3 4

be sure to tell our travel agents about it when we're all back home."

A few idiot grins, a round of sweaty handshakes, and we were back outside.

Jorgensen and I started down the staircase to the lobby in silence. Then he stopped and put a hand out toward me. "Ev," he said, "I've got a favor to ask. There's something I'd like you to do."

I hoped my answer would be a flat refusal, though I doubted it; turning down the man who controls the spigot on the golden calf never comes easy.

"After I tell the board where we stand, that they can't leave or even phone until this autopsy business is over—Oh, my God, how I dread this!—we've got to get the Oldses home. I'd like you to stay over an extra day or so, Ev, and take that job on."

"You mean chaperone this picnic and deliver one each, widow and coffin, to their doorstep?" I was incredulous. "I'll have to ask Jane first, see what she thinks about it."

"What's the matter, Franklin, afraid of your wife?"

I ignored that. "I'll let you know in the morning."

After breakfast the next morning, we spotted Jorgensen on the stairs leading up to the second landing. We charged up, two steps at a time. "No way," Jane said, without introduction. "I'm not going home alone. Either I stay here with Ev and leave with him, or else we both go home today."

"What about your boy?" the man asked weakly. "Don't you have to get back for him?"

"His father will be happy to take care of Billy," Jane said firmly. "That's what ex-husbands are for—I think."

Ed thought hard, and then said, "Okay, you two black-mailers win again. You both stay. Now here's how I see it. First off—"

"First off," Jane interrupted, "I think you should ask the Hollands if we can use the company plane they came down in. I don't like the idea very much of changing planes in Miami with a body in one hand and a hysterical woman in the other. And luggage in the third hand," she put in as an afterthought.

"How about San Juan?" Ed asked wryly. "You'd like changing there better, maybe? You're getting mighty bossy, Mrs. Franklin."

Jane looked him right in the eye. "Listen, Ed," she said, an edge to her ordinarily velvet voice, "you're damn right I am. I've had an awful lot of Elizabeth Olds since yesterday. I'm glad to help out, but she won't let either the Lamoureux or Holland women near her—not that Loretta Holland would dream of offering to do anything—and Dorothy Braun has completely chickened out. I think she's decided she's got to goddamn grade exams or something."

She put her hands on her hips, low down, like a motorcycle girl, pelvis thrust forward. "And she's been filling me full of how everybody on the island murdered her Henry, how she's going to put the corporation in a trust for her nephew's children so that even after she's gone there'll be nobody able to touch it, how the Hollands can whistle for any part of it, and how she hopes they string up George Lamoureux for the crook that he is before any of the Olds's money stays in his worthless bank, and so on into the night, in spite of enough Nembutal to knock out an elephant. And this morning again. Right now she's resting. But only to recharge the batteries, I'll bet, and once those sons of bitches are revved up again, she'll go on like a satellite goes on in orbit. Yeah, Ed, I'm getting bossy. You wanna know more about why?"

Ed eschewed any desire to know more. "I get the picture. You win. You stay with Ev, you both take Mrs. Olds home, I'll ask the Hollands about the plane, and if you decide you need your office repainted in off-shrimp I'll see what I can do. Oh, my God!"

"Good," Jane said, "and remember, I've got a witness." She eyed me critically. "For what he's worth, that is."

Caught between these two giants, I broke free. "Okay, let's get on with it. Ed, don't you need to let people know right away what the situation is? And to speak to Randy Holland?"

"Yeah. If they're all around the hotel I'll do it now. See you in a while." He strode off.

"You were magnificent, dear," I said to Jane.

"I know."

"Why didn't you ask for a raise while you were at it?"

"Maybe I should have. I could use the money."

"I meant for me, dummy."

She smiled, kissed me on the nose, put an arm around my waist, and started us down the last of the steps to the lobby. To a casual observer I imagine we would have looked like a couple of handsome newlyweds descending the grand staircase into the ballroom of the *Titanic,* carefree, very much in love, and ever so looking forward to come what may.

We saw Ed Jorgensen in earnest conversation with the Hollands, but before we could duck to one side, he waved us over, damn the man. Loretta Holland was speaking, the normal cool gone from her voice. "I don't see why we should. Of course it's a terrible thing that's happened, but I've run out of other cheeks to turn. I mean, after what she's said to me, why should we turn over the company plane? We were going over to Houston after this, Mr. Jorgensen, and I still intend to, and that's that."

"Ah, come on, Loretta," Randolph Holland urged, "the poor old cow is out of her mind. She's been popping sleeping pills like they was Hershey bars but she's still groaning up a storm like Lady Macbeth. We can afford to help out, can't we?"

I started to back away, since turning invisible was as yet beyond my powers. "Wait a minute, Ev," Jorgensen said. "Let's get this settled first." I stayed, though I don't know what purpose that served; as far as the Hollands were concerned I could have been bare-ass naked and squeezing pimples without their even noticing.

Loretta went on. "And after she's been so offensive? After she's said she'd never sell out to us? She knows how important it is to you right now. The woman is petty and vindictive and if you let her have the plane, I'll, I'll—" We never found out because the lady turned on her heel and walked out of the room.

A voice pierced the air, and Elizabeth Olds, batteries apparently mended, entered, looked about, and in tones more appropriate for a Handelian contralto, her voice poured forth: "Oh, Lord, you should have taken me instead." I doubt that she meant a word of it, but rather was unable to resist the opportunity to reproach the Almighty yet again for getting things wrong. She had, after all, looked about the room and counted the house before speaking.

"Oh, damn," Jane whispered, and she went over to lead the lady to a chair. "Sit down here, Mrs. Olds, and we'll see about getting you something to eat. You've got to keep up your strength," she added, though the remark might as appropriately have been made to a raging bull.

"I think you ought to go over too," I said to Ed Jorgensen. "It's your place." I didn't add that it was also his place to relieve Jane at the helm, though we both knew that was what I meant.

He shot me a look of purest loathing, but he complied. "Dear Mrs. Olds," he crooned in a voice that fit him like a Bing Crosby imitation fits a punk rock star, "this will all be over soon. The hospital will be releasing Mr. Olds's—Mr. Olds very shortly, and we'll see that you and he are taken home. Ev Franklin here will be going with you. And out of respect for Mr. Olds, we've cancelled the rest of our meeting," he added, deftly concealing the fact that this was a spur of the moment decision. After all, what was there to lose? If the surviving members of the board were too upset to sleep during the sessions, the whole affair would be a disaster anyway.

Elizabeth Olds looked up sharply at Jorgensen. Then her eyes went blurry again. To everyone's surprise she boomed, "I should fucking well hope so," and then she conked out again. Jane caught her as she slumped floorward. I don't think she was herself. Or maybe, for one of the few times in her life, she was indeed herself. Or maybe they were including a fascinating new ingredient in with the Nembutal.

Out of respect for Henry Olds, as Ed Jorgensen had said, the meetings were called off. Everybody went to worship in his or her own way. Most of the mourners conducted services on the golf course. Jane and I went to the beach. Elizabeth Olds, as I noticed looking in a window as we passed, went to the dining room.

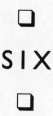

SIX

We swam. We floated on the water and turned our faces to the sun, the warm, relaxing, life-giving sun, and skin cancer be damned. "Ev," Jane said, "after we're terribly rich, do you suppose we could buy a little piece of something like this in addition to the apple orchard?"

"Of course. As soon as we pick the first golden apple. If gold is four hundred fifty an ounce and an apple weighs about ten ounces, that's—well, maybe after the first half dozen golden apples."

"Fair enough. And we give up Manhattan altogether, right?"

"Right." We were both tired of Madison Avenue, hysteria, and living in buildings that, according to the style of the moment, had lobbies decorated in mock Art Deco or pseudo Anne Hathaway's cottage or fake Shibui conversation pit;

buildings with elevators that even in the best of circumstances smelled suspiciously like powder rooms for doggies and small children. "But for now, let's eat. There's a stand down there where we can grab a hot dog or a burger."

We walked at the water's edge. We picked up the occasional sea shell or stone and considered taking them back home, but ended by tossing the shells into the water and skimming the stones across the surface. After all, when they've dried off and lost their shine, or when they've joined the other shells and stones in a box on the hall closet shelf, who is there who hasn't wondered why the hell he or she brought them back home in the first place?

We munched happily on our junk food and sipped soft drinks out of cans. "Let's go down see if they're working on the commercial," Jane mumbled through a mouthful of a soft, tooth-destroying bun. "And then let's get out of the sun."

When we found them, the TV crew was taking a break. Carlla and Ken were sitting under an umbrella looking at the script. Walking up to them, I said, "Don't tell me there are lines to learn! What won't they think of next?"

"Don't get excited," Carlla said. "All I do is trail a quarter of a mile of chiffon and gallop around a palm tree. No talking. Anyway, there's been enough talking for a month around here today."

"Oh, Lord, has there ever!" Ken said. "Madam Olds passed by like the voice of doom. Jane, darling, I thought you were supposed to keep her tethered in her stall."

Jane let that one pass with a weary sigh.

"What's she been saying?" I asked.

"Nothing much," Carlla explained. "Only that every third visitor in this lousy swamp killed her husband. Listen, why doesn't the old girl cut it out? I'd even consider feeling sorry for her if she'd give us half a chance. Look. Henry was an old man, and he was a sick man. He used to show me his pill collection, and he was sort of proud of it, you know? And he didn't complain. Even made a joke out of it sometimes. The doctors told him he was too old for a hernia operation, and then he told me he was building a special wing on the house

for his collection of trusses. I mean, that's a ballsy old guy."
A bittersweet smile crossed her face, a smile that was sad and
happy all at the same time.

"Hey, that's it!" Ken shouted. "You give me that smile for
the next take and every forty-year-old broad in America will
be pouring her Clairol down the toilet, I guarantee yuh!"

"I will not," Jane muttered, speaking to no one in particular.

But Ken had his priorities in the right order. A happy smile
may bring warmth to the heart, but a happy client puts the
Scotch salmon into the Sunday brunch.

"She threatens everybody, is all," Carlla went on, ignoring
Ken's interruption. "We're all guilty, I think, so long as we're
here and we're breathing. Listen, if anybody did kill Henry
Olds, which I doubt, he'd be nuts not to do a follow-up job on
Henry's wife. I can be sympathetic only so far and then I'm
going to tie that broad's tits in a knot, she doesn't shut up."
The explosion over, she sprang to her feet and walked off.

Ken looked after her. "Poor darling," he explained to Jane
and me. "She's upset."

"We'll leave," Jane said. "Talking about this isn't going to
do her any good. And you've got your work to get through."

We started off. "Thank you, duckies," Ken called out. "See
you later."

We trudged back toward the hotel. As we passed one of the
cottages for the fine folk, one facing the water, we heard a
female voice raised in a shrill tone somewhere between fury
and tears. It was just recognizable as Dolly Lamoureux's un-
ladylike howling. "How dare you! Get out of here, you,
you—"

Another voice, a male voice, mumbled. We couldn't hear
what it was saying, and I instinctively veered left to get nearer
to the action. Jane looked at me cynically. "Nosey bastard,"
she whispered. But she came along too.

"That's right," I agreed softly. "Now you know. Shhh!"

"Don't you dare accuse me of anything!" Mrs. L continued.
"Get out of here, you impudent—you, you!"

The door opened, and a man came out. It was the bartender who had served us coffee and drinks at the board meeting. He was in a hurry; his head down, looking neither right nor left, he scooted back in the direction of the main building.

"Well, what do you know!" I said to Jane.

Dolly wasn't finished yet. Now she was hooting into the horn. "Let me speak to the manager. Immediately, do you hear! . . . This is Mrs. George Lamoureux in Cottage 8 . . . Yes . . . One of your people had the audacity to come into the cottage just now and accuse me," she shrieked, "accuse me of—" Apparently with a sudden awareness that she was eminently audible, she dropped her voice abruptly, and all we could hear after that was an unpleasant shrilling, the music without the words.

"Damn!" I said.

"You're better off not knowing," Jane said. "I don't want you borrowing trouble, you hear?"

I said I heard, and I thought I heard, but I guess maybe I hadn't heard, or if I had it didn't make much difference in what happened later.

SEVEN

That evening Ed Jorgensen, Jane, and I had dinner together. We included Elizabeth Olds in our group, which may have been the decent thing to do, but certainly wasn't much fun. The lady had calmed down some and had put her accusations of murder into a lower key. She also managed to shovel in sufficient fodder to stoke a dray horse. But then, why not?

Conversation was desultory, to say the most.

Jane asked, "Have you seen the new Masterpiece Theater series on public television, Mrs. Olds?"

Silverware clanked.

"No, I haven't." Silence followed.

"It's quite good," I offered.

"Henry and I almost never turned the TV on." Mrs. Olds sighed, as if realizing yet again that the fun of almost never turning the TV on with Henry was a thing of the past.

More silverware clanked. Jane didn't try again, and I could tell from the set expression on her face that she figured someone else, preferably Ed Jorgensen, could get the ball rolling if he wanted to. He didn't. "Do you have decaffeinated coffee?" was the most trenchant remark of the next half hour, with the possible exception of Elizabeth Olds's pronouncement: "Waiter, this fork is filthy!"

As we got up to leave, the captain came over and murmured discreetly. "If it is convenient for the lady," he whispered, "Sarge would like a few words with Mrs. Olds and your party in the lounge. This way, please."

We were ushered into a side room off the lobby. Sarge stood to greet us. He was dressed more formally for the evening, with a long-sleeved shirt this time, though the buttons didn't quite make it over that belly button, which I thought leered concupiscently at the grieving widow.

"Dear Mrs. Olds," he said, "please do sit. And allow me to express my condolences. Gentlemen, ladies, please seat yourselves. I'll try to be brief."

For all his sympathy and undisputed charm, Sarge was no more capable of eliciting a response from Mrs. Olds than the rest of us. She sat, remaining upright on the edge of her cushioned wicker chair, clutching her precious bag of knitting, while the rest of us leaned back and waited.

"Our examination of Mr. Olds is complete," Sarge said delicately, "and on one point at least I can offer some small comfort. Your husband was not deliberately, ah, deliberately dispatched, madam. The gentleman suffered a massive coronary occlusion. Speaking for the government of San Sebo, I can only say we regret this deeply and offer you our sincere sympathy."

Elizabeth Olds was not one to be put off by a mere dictator, and she still had sufficient reserves to rise to the occasion. "Poppycock," she said. "He was murdered. I assume this charade is over and I can take my husband home. I intend to. And I intend to have another examination in the Olds Memorial hospital, and we'll find out what happened soon enough." She stood, and as she did so she seemed to dwarf even Sarge. She turned and marched off. Rolling drums and snarling trumpets would not have been out of place.

Sarge wasn't accustomed to contradiction. This time *he* stood. "If this woman slanders my people, the government of San Sebo will have the United States before the World Court in the Hague. You won't find us as easy to deal with as Nicaragua! And if we get no satisfaction there, you can expect me to address the United Nations. This is racism, pure and simple." He raised a finger to the sky. "Genocide!" He marched out. Reprise for drums and trumpets.

The three of us looked at each other wearily. Should we laugh, cry, or get drunk? "Anybody got any ideas?" Ed asked.

"If we could get a fourth," Jane suggested, "maybe we could play bridge."

"I don't play," I said.

We began laughing, though none of us knew for sure at what.

❏

EIGHT

❏

"Come on into the bar, you two," Ed Jorgensen said. "This calls for a celebration. If Finch, Rowan, & Hyde is going to be denounced before the Security Council, every agency in the country'll be green with envy. Dom Perignon, I think, and we'll charge it to the board."

While we were sipping the champagne, Loretta Holland made an entrance. The soft lights of the bar were caught in her blonde hair and in the silver of her dress. Strategic spots on her wrist and around her neck glistened with an equal passion.

She looked about, her head turning slowly, chin raised regally, as if she were following a screen director's orders to enter with presence and command. Having accomplished this with total success she approached our table. "Good evening," she said with a polite if impersonal smile. "I hoped I'd find you here."

I felt vaguely guilty, as if her hope of finding me in the bar was based on some poorly concealed flaw in my character.

"I want to talk to you about Mrs. Olds. About getting her home, I mean. I've talked it over with Randy, and he's convinced me that we ought to let her have the plane. I don't have to tell you what I think of Elizabeth Olds, but under the circumstances . . . Well, she's been through a lot, I suppose. Randy has talked to the pilot, and after he deposits the lady and the coffin he'll trundle back for us. We'll take a few extra days here. Without," she added in an expressionless tone, "the presence of the rest of the board."

"That's very kind of you," Ed said. "and if I can speak for Mrs. Olds, I thank you for a very generous gesture."

"You're very welcome, Mr. Jorgensen. Someday, perhaps Mrs. Olds will speak for herself, though I doubt it. Well, Randy is waiting for me in the room, so I'll excuse myself now. Good evening." She smiled, turned and looked about the room in the same regal way, and made her exit. And believe me, making an exit is very different from merely exiting.

The three of us were true to form in our reactions:

"Wasn't that nice!" Jorgensen the practical said.

"What a bitch!" Jane the honest observed.

"Oh, I dunno," Franklin the waffler offered.

When the bottle had been drained, Ed said he had some work to do in his room. As his research director, I felt reasonably certain that the man merely needed to get away and forget about the mess we were in. There was a research study some years ago about top executives who took work home or on vacation, and it turned out that while over 90 percent of them did so at least once a month, only 10 percent actually got around to opening those expensive top-grain leather dispatch cases and extracting the contents. Taking work out of the office makes a responsible executive feel dedicated; doing something with it is another matter. But who am I to enlighten my own boss about his behavior? "Okay, Ed," I said, "don't work too hard."

"I'll look in on Elizabeth Olds," Jane said. "Then I'll probably read in the lounge for a while. Why don't you take a walk on the beach or something, Ev?"

"That's just what I'll do. I'll be back when it gets dark."

The three of us went our separate ways. I walked along the water's edge, just above the point where the highest waves made their final surge up onto the shore. The sand was packed down by the water, and walking was easy. I took off my shoes and socks, gave my trousers a turn up, and set off, feeling the sand through my toes and looking at my footprints. My arches looked as if they might be getting flat. I made a mental note to see a podiatrist. Or something.

There was a fisherman down the way, and when I got close I saw that he was sitting on a stool by the boat he had pulled up on the shore, and was busily mending his net. "Good evening," I said.

"Good evening to you, sir," he replied. "Are you enjoying your stay in San Sebo?"

"It's a beautiful island," I answered, avoiding the question.

He grinned. "Yes, it is. Thank you. And that was a delicate response to my question."

I was startled. "What? I, uh, you've just surprised me, you know."

"It's all right, sir. I did it on purpose. It was mean of me." He explained. "I was educated in the States, and spent some years there when I was young."

In the half-light, I had paid no attention to his appearance, but I could see now, from his weathered skin, the wrinkles in his neck, the grizzled, tight curls on his head, that he was far from young. It's difficult to estimate the age of someone who is not only of another race but has in addition lived a different life from one's own, in this case a life on a tropical island in the Caribbean Sea, a life with cares, fears, hopes, and joys that I couldn't even guess at, much less comprehend.

"Oh, I see. And now, you live here on San Sebo, and you, uh—"

"Don't be embarrassed. Now I live here on San Sebo, and now I'm a fisherman. It's a peaceful life for an old man. More or less, anyway. And call me Doc, Mr. Franklin. Everybody calls me Doc.''

"You know my name?''

"Your party is famous. A death, accusations, glamorous rich people from the world of television—this is all very special for us. And there is much illiteracy here. The news goes by word of mouth. In this case it goes out from the hotel by way of the serving staff and across the island to all San Sebo. Shall I tell you what the lady whose husband died said to the other ladies?''

"I'll take your word for it, Doc.'' I wondered what a poor man like this, what all the poor people on the island, thought of the tourists who must look so unbelievably, so unfairly rich, sated with beautiful clothes and even more beautiful food, and so carelessly accepting of it all. I asked. "Tell me, Doc, what do the Seboans think about us tourists. We've got so much, they've got so little, and unlike you, I don't imagine many of them have had the chance to see what life is really like back in the States. They only see us here as rich people, as the owners of the earth. What do they think?''

He thought for a moment, picking at a ravelled piece of rope on his net, deciding it was good enough for another day, and moving on to another bit. "I think,'' he said slowly, "I think they decide not to think. It's a job, it's a living.''

He was being discreet, choosing his words carefully. He went on. "I can only talk about myself. And I find that difficult. It's different all the time, at every age. When I was a small child, the tourists would smile at me and say I was cute. They'd give me candy, cakes. Sometimes a lady would pick me up and hug me. Then when I was a young man and looked at them differently, some of them would still smile. And some of them would do more than that.''

He lowered his work and looked up at me. "I had some very good times in those days with the tourist ladies. One of them still sends me presents. A box of cigars every Christmas. Sarge takes half of them—he calls it customs duties—and I keep the rest. But of course I can't say anything or the cigars would most likely stop coming altogether. She must be an old lady by now, a very elderly party, just like me." He paused, memories filling his eyes. "Then when I was middle-aged, and not so attractive any more, I would still look at the ladies, but they would either look through me—I was part of the scenery, one of the amenities of the island, you know?—or else they would turn away haughtily. I knew, because I had been to the mainland, that most of them were just ordinary people, but here they were the lords of the earth, and they could turn away haughtily and believe in what they were doing.

"Well, after that, I got old. You know how I knew I was getting old?" I shook my head. "It was because they started to smile at me again, the ladies. I was past the time of being a threat. I was atmosphere and local color again, the way I was as a child. I was part of the vacation, part of what they had paid for. I'm not sure I've answered your question, but that's all I can say."

"Doc, what in hell did you do in the States?"

"Oh, this and that. I went to school there."

"And studied—what?"

He bent down to his net again. "Just school, Mr. Franklin. That's all, just school."

I had been dismissed; the interview was concluded; there was no point in pressing on. "Well, it's been good to talk to you. I'm leaving tomorrow," I said, "and I won't see you again. I wish you well, Doc. It's a pleasure to have met you."

"Thank you, Mr. Franklin. And as your President Johnson used to say, 'Come back and see us again, you hear?' And enjoy your ride in Mr. Holland's plane."

He couldn't control his grin as he said that last. Was there nothing he didn't know about what went on in San Sebo?

I walked back to the hotel to pick up Jane, but the lounge was empty. Out of idle curiosity—Jane says I give new meaning to the term old woman—I went to the desk and asked if I could speak to the man who had been our bartender. I thought I might get a little inside information on what went on in Dolly Lamoureux's room to upset her so. "I forgot to tip the man, what with all the excitement," I explained.

"Oh, that's Jackie," the desk clerk said with a smile. "One moment, sir." She disappeared into the office, and came back in a moment with the grin wiped off.

With her was the manager. "I appreciate the gesture," he said, "but we don't allow tipping."

"You don't? This must be the only hotel in the world not to allow tipping. Congratulations." He gave a deprecatory nod. "But I'd like to speak to the man, anyway. Can you send him to my room?"

"It's a little awkward, sir, but I'm not even sure which man was on duty with you. Perhaps tomorrow?"

"The young lady here said it was Jackie. Is Jackie around now?"

"I didn't say nothin'," the girl protested. "Nothin' a-tall."

"Thank you, Maryann," the manager said. "You can go now. I'll be here until Glenna comes on duty. Go ahead, now!" he said to the clerk, stricken rigid by the unheard of early release from duty. He turned and favored me with that bland manager smile they learn so quickly. "I'm so sorry, sir. The help we get these days! Jackie hasn't been with us for months. Perhaps tomorrow?" he asked hopefully.

I was getting nowhere. But at least I knew there was somewhere I should be getting, so I decided to drop it for now and try another approach in the morning. "Okay," I said, "thanks anyway," and I left to return to the cottage and Jane.

□

NINE

□

No such luck. Early the next morning Ed Jorgensen called with two pieces of information. First, he himself was at the airport about to wing his way north, happy as a Canada goose and twice as messy. And Henry Olds's body was released for shipping home. Mrs. Olds was packing everything, save for several dozen imprecations she was lavishing with indiscriminate affection on everyone within earshot, the pilot was dressing, and there were very likely bevies of native girls weaving garlands of something Hawaiian to drape about us as we embarked. The Franklin family's escort services were urgently requested.

"Aloha, and all that," I said to Jane. "I'll be happy to get this over with."

"Okay, let's pack. A trip like this, I don't think I'll even cop an ashtray for a souvenir. I'd rather forget it."

Out of long years of practice, we packed in moments, called a bellman, and were through the door. I forgot all about Jackie the bartender, or not-Jackie the bartender, as the case might have been. We were shuttled over to the little airport and embarked. Mrs. Olds had boarded before us, as had Henry's mortal remains, there in the center aisle, there being no luggage compartment big enough for a coffin. The pilot was in the passenger cabin to greet us, oblivious of the glare from Elizabeth Olds as he set his coffee down on the coffin to do so. Frankly, short of balancing it on his head or asking the lady to hold it for him, I don't know what else he could have done, but I suppose to the widow it looked like another slap at her, not from the Hollands this time, but from one of their minions. And I know she envisaged a stain, a ring on the coffin for all eternity, a flaw in the perfection she had ordained.

We settled in our seats and fastened the belts. The pilot returned to the cockpit, the engines roared. We taxied over to the runway, the engines roared again, and we were off. Way off. Before we had even reached the end of the runway, and just after we began to feel the smooth glide that goes with lifting off the ground, the roar was replaced by a sputter, a sputter that grew worse with each advancing mini-second, and that ended with our dropping earthward just as we cleared a small fishing smack in San Sebo's harbor. More precisely, we dropped waterward, though I was not personally aware of the impact, having had my head knocked about on the back of the seat in front.

Later, I thought I recalled the coffin scooting down the aisle at the moment of the crash, at the same time that my head was being propelled forward. I wondered if the contents thereof were showing yellowed teeth in one last opportunity to upset those present by careening forward at breakneck speed. On the other hand, I'm not entirely sure; I may have made that memory up out of whole cloth.

I do remember, however, being fished out. The plane remained afloat for a decent interval, appearing to take more easily to a watery element than to the air, and with the exception of the late Mr. Olds, we made our several ways out of the elegance of the Holland corporate plane into the garbagey depths of what had to be San Sebo's municipal dump. For a while I was intimately involved with several abominations the precise nature of which I was, fortunately, too much in shock to be able to ascertain.

At first I was only numb, but gradually I became aware that something was happening to my leg. It felt as if a six-inch sliver of glass had been jammed into the bone above my left knee, driven down through the knee itself, and finally anchored in the bone below. It felt as if the surface of my leg had then been miraculously healed so that nothing showed, and the pain was all locked on the inside. It felt like hell.

We were taken to the hospital. Jane and Mrs. Olds were released almost immediately. The pilot had suffered a concussion and had to remain. I was diagnosed as having achieved something with a grandiose title, thrombophlebitis, which required bed rest, an elastic bandage, and more quiet than I was likely to get, in order to avoid the formation of a blood clot on the left knee. The hospital was a reasonably relaxed institution, so I had only minor objections to make.

"Just you and the pilot," Jane observed. "Like I've always told you, girls are tougher than boys. In addition to being more reliable."

"Thanks," I said. "I'll remember that next time you want me to cut up a tree for the cabin."

"There are different kinds of strength," Jane replied. "Some of them you got."

"Enough. What about the body?"

"What about it? It's fine, I guess. I never thought to ask, to be truthful. I mean, what more can happen to it?" She saw me rise up in a feeble attempt to show exasperation. "Okay, okay. Keep cool. The body is still in the harbor, when last I tuned in. Frankly, Ev," she said, turning serious, "I've been too concerned about you to ask. You kept fading in and out all day, you know."

"I did?"

"You sure did, kid. But they tell me you're going to be

okay, so long as you keep off your feet for a little while. The hospital looks like a pretty good place, as these things go. You know it's a training hospital for kids mostly from back home. And when they release you, the hotel management wants to put us up until you're completely better. Gratis. I said we'd love to stay on a bit."

"That's great. You think we can stay for free and still put it on the expense account?" Larceny is the spice of life, at least on Madison Avenue.

"Why not? If Ed Jorgensen doesn't snoop around too much, anyway."

"Hey, listen, what the hell happened with that damn plane?"

"Don't know yet. Maybe when the pilot clears out of the fog he's in we can find out."

"You know, Jane, there's something awfully fishy going on around here. And if we've got to stay anyway—"

And that's how I got myself involved this time. I sometimes think I'm like that comic strip character that used to go around with a small rain cloud over his head all the time, even on sunny days. Especially on sunny days.

□

TEN

□

And now it was Tuesday. The board meetings had sunk into history as triumphantly as Holland's plane had plopped into the harbor, but a number of the participants were still around. Jane and I were waiting for my knee to heal; the Hollands were arranging for another corporate plane since Loretta fancied commercial airlines the same way she fancied cattle cars; the Lamoureuxs were expecting a sailboat they had chartered in advance to take them around the Caribbean and then to San Juan; the television crew had a few days' work left to complete; and Elizabeth Olds was still recovering from her second shock of the week. And nobody was talking to nobody, everybody being furious with everybody, which by my standards showed common sense and good taste all around.

By Wednesday Big Ed had sent me a CARE package from home. How he had found out about my hospital stay I have no idea, but everywhere there are spies. Unhappy at my languishing in bed, he had seen to it that the results of a study we had done for a brokerage house client were instantly enplaned in my direction. Whether this was to keep me in good mental health or to keep me earning my salary even while horizontal, is a question not to be asked lest an answer be forthcoming.

Sighing deeply, I picked up the heavy set of interviews with respondents who owned stocks and bonds and had incomes over $50,000. You may have seen the TV commercial one brokerage house has been airing for several seasons, in which a virile and authoritative voice proclaims, "Minds Over Money." Our problem was simple: What the hell did a meaningless phrase like that mean, and why the hell was it successful, and could anything be developed for our client that would work as well?

Jane was of the opinion that Minds Over Money meant what it said—their minds, your money, and them all over what was yours. After I had gone through the material Jorgensen had sent I realized Jane was wrong. The meaningless phrase meant precisely that—nothing—and that was what it was meant to mean. Or to not mean. That answered the first question.

As to why it was successful, the interviews in depth gave out some very strong hints. They threw that firm, manly voice at all us fearful investors so that our little heads would be filled with mental pictures of dear old dad telling us what to do, saying, "Son, (or daughter), for your own good I'm telling you to dig into your pocket and hand over all your cash before you lose it. You know you're not to be trusted to take care of it properly, but Daddy knows what to do. Daddy knows best. Now fork it over, my child." And you do. And the advertiser's sales and profits and number of accounts climb up and up.

The third problem, to decide what Finch, etc.'s, client could do to cut off a piece of the action for itself, was more difficult. It took me all of Wednesday to figure it out, and then only because Jane got in the act with me, but we did it.

First I called my office in New York to have someone look up some census statistics, and then we planned the strategy.

Grinning along with Jane in triumph, I grabbed the bedside phone and called New York again. "Hey, Bill," I said to the account man, "I have a line on your problem with the brokerage account. Big Ed sent the research poop down and Jane and I have just finished going over it."

The phone mumbled its gratitude and I continued. "The thing is," I explained, "the competition is appealing to emotions, not to reason. They're calming the frightened investors down. They're telling people to relax and leave it to dear old dad, and he'll make everything be all right."

"So what do we do," old Bill asked, "tell them dad's a worthless bum, not to listen to the old lush?"

"Wait a minute, willya? First, do you know that the census shows way over half the women in the country are in the work force? And that women control a tremendous share of the national bank balance? And that this is getting bigger every day?"

"So now I know. Now what?"

Account men can be so dull. "Don't you see? Momma's going to be the authority figure on investments any day now, and the competition has overlooked that. You need a mother image saying the equivalent of Minds Over Money to grab off the market the other guy's neglected."

There was a squawk out of the phone. "Come on," I replied, "of course you can't say it like that. You've got to do even better. Something maybe like, 'Hand it over, sonny, and watch mommy make it grow bigger.' That'd get the kids who look on mother as the family authority figure, and it wouldn't be too bad with the Oedipus complex crowd either."

The phone jabbered like a tape of a henhouse when the chief cock of the barnyard walks in. Played at double speed at that. "Look, Bill," I complained, "figuring out how to say it without the Feds cracking down is your job, not mine. I just provide the operational framework; you fill in the details, willya, and leave me out of it." I hung up.

"Account men can be so ungrateful," I said to Jane. I made a sour face, but the truth was that I felt much better than I had in days, ready to leave my sickbed and face life.

Thursday afternoon the hospital sprang me. Proud of their first rate equipment they gave me a spanking new motorized wheelchair, about as useful for propelling myself about the local terrain as a dog sled. I used it in the hotel lobby, however, to enhance my celebrity status among the hotel guests. They also gave me a pair of crutches, which made more sense, plus a warning not to use them. I couldn't figure it out, but Jane decided that the hospital administrator had taken a course back in the States on how to cover your tail in case a patient institutes a malpractice suit.

I spent a fat ten minutes in bed in our cottage, and then, driven by boredom, I trucked over to the lobby where I wheeled around in my motorized toy until boredom returned, which took perhaps three minutes, finally screeching to a halt in front of the main desk. "Is Jackie the bartender around?" I asked.

This time the desk clerk had been properly briefed. "He don't work here no more, sir."

"Oh? When did he leave?"

"I think it was two, three months ago, sir."

Ask a foolish question, get a foolish answer. I zoomed over to the entry, grabbed my crutches, and set out on a hobble down the beach, hospital warnings or no. My new friend Doc should be back from fishing, and maybe he'd be interested in a tad of gossip.

He was on the beach, working on his net again. "Hello, Mr. Franklin, you shouldn't be on your feet, you know. They told you that at the hospital, didn't they? You don't want a blood clot, do you, now?"

"Doc, is there anything you don't know about this island?"

He smiled. "You can try me. I'd like to know the answer to that question myself."

"Okay. Let's begin with a man who works at the hotel. Jackie. He's a bartender. Do you know about him?"

"Oh, I know everybody on the island, but that's no trick.

We're all cousins here. Only I'm surprised you know about Jackie. I think he left San Sebo. Months ago, I think."

I dropped it. Whatever was going on, was going on, and I wasn't supposed to know about it. There wasn't any reason I should expect Doc to break ranks and level with me. "Okay, then tell me what's new around here."

"So. Now that's something I *can* do. Did you know that your Mrs. Lamoureux has taken your Mrs. Olds for a little picnic?" I shook my head. "Yes, she has indeed. There's a pleasant lagoon on the other side of the island from the harbor, and they set out about one this afternoon with a picnic basket. To cheer Mrs. Olds up, I think. Both the ladies took their knitting and sat there, hardly saying a single word to each other. Just the clickety clack of their knitting needles. I tell you, Mr. Franklin, that's not the way we Seboans have a good time for ourselves, no sir."

"That's interesting," I said, even though it wasn't. To myself I added a thought about Dolly Lamoureux, the poor chubby, that fading baby face first looking anxiously at Henry Olds, trying to cotton up in order to save her husband, and now trying the same tactic on that stony relict Elizabeth. And I guessed that she would have kept pushing down the certain knowledge that she had about as much chance of moving Elizabeth Olds as she had of moving the island of San Sebo farther out to sea.

"Oh, but wait. The next thing anybody knew Mrs. Lamoureux was back in the town, rushing to the hospital. Many people saw her, and there was quite a bit of gossip."

"You mean she just left Mrs. Olds out there, and—did you say the hospital? My God, what happened? Is Mrs. Olds all right?" It didn't seem credible that Elizabeth Olds would do anything drastic, like have a try at suicide, and even less likely was the idea that she might have been taken ill.

Doc grinned. "Oh, this is something you find more interesting. Well, wait a moment, Mr. Franklin, it gets even more perplexing. Mrs. Lamoureux went to the hospital, but not because of Mrs. Olds. She went there to see her husband. She said she had received a note out at the lagoon that her husband had been taken ill and that she was needed immediately. But nobody at the hospital knew about it, and they finally located Mr. Lamoureux, safe and sound, dozing under a palm tree on the beach."

"What's going on, Doc? Why would anybody play a trick like that?"

"That's a good question, Mr. Franklin, and it's not the only one: Who would play a trick like that, and where is the note? Mrs. Lamoureux says she doesn't have it, and neither does anybody else. It's all very mysterious, isn't it?"

I shook my head. "I don't get it. There's something fishy. I think I'd better get back. Thanks for the information."

"Not at all, sir. And if you learn anything, perhaps you wouldn't mind sharing it with an old fisherman?"

I said I wouldn't mind, but I had the distinct notion that if I learned anything it would be a minimum of two hours after the old fisherman had learned it for himself.

"Good-bye for now then, Doc," I said. "I need to get off this leg. Maybe I'll see you again before I leave. I hope so."

"Oh, no no, no. How stupid I am, letting you stand on that leg. You come sit awhile. My house is just a few yards from here off the beach."

"I'd love to," the old lady in me said, never averse to a chance to snoop. But at least I resolved not to run a white glove over the window sills to see how much dust I could pick up.

I hobbled along with Doc at my side until we reached a modest bungalow. Doc pulled a canvas chair into the shade and instructed me to sit. Without asking, he brought me a ginger beer. "This will pick you up," he said, and then he turned and called to a young woman hanging out her wash to the side of the house. "Juleen," he called, "come and meet our guest. And bring little Andy." He explained to me: "Juleen is my niece, and little Andy is her boy. Her husband was big Andy. But unfortunately"—he spread his hands helplessly—"he was killed a while back. When the American patrol boat fired into the town, you know?"

"Oh, I'm sorry."

By that time Juleen was with us and heard me. She smiled. "It's not your fault, sir. You're Mr. Franklin," she announced. "I'm pleased to meet you. And this is little Andy." She rubbed the shoulder of the small child, perhaps ten years old, who was leaning against her shyly.

"You know my name?" I asked. I should have known better; not a sparrow fell to earth on San Sebo without the tomtoms and the smoke signals taking note. "And how are you, young fellow? What've you got there? You've been drawing pictures! Come here, Andy, and let me see." I always feel like such a damned hypocrite babbling to kids; I hadn't the slightest interest in his scribblings, but I felt obligated, the same way I feel I have to jump into that over-chlorinated swimming pool and burn my eyes out when a friend is kind enough to invite me to the health club he's so proud of.

I looked at the pictures the child had been drawing on scraps of old paper, the other sides of which indicated they had been salvaged from Seboan junk piles. There were landscapes, palm trees, portraits of women carrying bundles on their heads. The scenes of normal life on a tiny island. They were incredibly good, and one in particular, a picture of what I judged to be a fighting cock, had almost the same demented power and thrust as a Picasso cock.

"Hey, Andy," I said, "little Andy. Would you like to let me buy that rooster from you? I'd sure like to have it. How about a dollar?"

The child was tongue-tied. His mother answered for him. "No, mister, that's too much. Twenty-five cents is what we charges the tourists for little Andy's pictures."

"If you really want to do something for the boy," Doc said, "and I'm embarrassed at asking, he sure could use some paper."

"Paper?"

"What can I tell you? It's hard to get. There's just a little for the school, and then for the tourists and the government and the hospital, but otherwise, I know it sounds strange, but it's a low priority import. Food comes first. So the boy gets scraps, mostly from the hotels and the hospital. Not from the government because Sarge likes to make believe such things don't happen, and the clerks are afraid to take anything out for him."

"Of course. I'll get some hotel stationery before I leave. And," I said directly to the boy, "I'll get you fresh paper, clean on both sides. You come to my cottage at nine tomorrow morning and I'll have it. You're a real talent, son. You keep at it, you hear?" To my horror, I really meant it, and wasn't just making awkward talk to some kid. Andy must have found it mawkish, though, because he buried his face in his mother's skirt again.

"You know the lady, that big lady?" the boy asked me in a timid voice.

"Which lady is that, Andy?" I asked.

He frowned. "I don't know." Apparently all tourist ladies looked alike, which is an interesting switch on things back home. I wondered if in about fifteen years he would turn to a companion and remark, "But they're cute when they're young." He looked up and brightened. "The big lady who fight. I could draw her good, she let me."

The three adults laughed. "They all fight, Andy." I stood, with an assist from Doc. "Well, I'm off now, or my wife will wonder where I am. Good to have met you all. Take care."

Doc raised a hand in farewell. "Arrivederla," he said, rolling the r's in the best Italian style.

That did it. I stopped and turned toward him again. "Look, Doc," I said, "there's something I want to ask you." He nodded. "Everybody on this island speaks the same, except for two people, you and—"

"Sarge. Sarge and me." He laughed.

"That's it, you and Sarge. I know you went to school in the States, but what's the story with Sarge? Sometimes he sounds like Winston Churchill telling people he's not going to preside over the dissolution of the king's empire. Can you tell me about it?"

"You've said it yourself, or come close to it, anyway. When Sarge was a very young man, and the English still ran San Sebo, there wasn't much a bright, ambitious boy could do about having a future. He could maybe get a job with the

6 4

little bureaucracy that ran the island, or he could leave for somewhere else and hope for the best. Not that it's much different now.

"Well, Sarge was smart and good-looking and eager to please, and the governor and his wife took a fancy to him. They pushed him along as far as possible, which wasn't very far, and then, to make a long story short, he was sent to England for training. Training to set up a constabulary in San Sebo, training against the day that everybody knew would be coming soon when the British would be leaving and we'd be on our own, more or less."

"Uh huh," I said, "I get it, I think. So Sarge picked up a little bit of an English accent and began to think of himself as the ruling class, is that it?"

"It's more complicated than that, Mr. Franklin." Doc frowned thoughtfully. "Look at it this way. Sarge isn't a bad man, not really. But he's had a big problem. He's torn in half. He sometimes thinks he's an English gentleman trying to bring civilization to an island of children, savages, if you like. Then he looks at himself in the mirror and sees that shiny black skin, that flat nose against his face and he knows that he's one of the savages himself. And he knows he's got to be on our side, whether he likes it or not. The man doesn't know where he belongs; he hates us, in a way, because we're not like him, and he hates himself because he's not like them, the English. And then, to complete the picture, since he's not crazy—far from it—he has to face it: He's us and we're him, and he's got to take care of us if he wants to take care of himself.

"Do you understand? As I say, Sarge isn't a bad man, even though he does some bad things from time to time. Now I think I've said enough."

"Enough to give me a lot to think about, Doc. Thank you."

"You're very welcome. I don't think I have to ask you to keep this conversation private, just between the two of us."

"Believe me, I will. And good-bye again." I raised my hand and headed back to the hotel.

ELEVEN

There was a note on the bed. "All hell loose. Eliz O missing. Dolly Lam under arrest. Come to lobby."

Our little band, for once united, was gathered around George Lamoureux and extending comfort. Even Loretta Holland.

"Don't you worry," Randolph Holland was saying, "they can't do anything to her. This is a lot of nonsense."

"Bunch of savages throwing their weight around," Loretta said, "but they're smart enough to know they can't get away with it. Randy can get this into half a dozen newspapers by morning. They'll be changing their tune, you'll see."

George Lamoureux looked unimpressed. "God knows what these people can do. How the hell can they accuse Dolly of murder? They're insane! Why would she want to? And even if she wanted to, I mean, Dolly's a timid woman." His shoulders slumped. "Damn them. Damn them, anyway."

Jane drew me aside. "They found Mrs. Olds," she whispered. "In the lagoon. Dead. Floating."

"What happened?"

"Who knows? The barracuda had been at her. I identified her, and it was awful, Ev. The poor woman was, her legs were, oh, Ev, she was almost—shredded!" Her voice rose, and she pulled herself back to a lower volume. "She could have been swimming, she could have been cut while she was still on shore, either on purpose or by accident, and then pushed in. In that case the blood would have drawn the damn fish. Hell, nobody can tell, and I don't see what they hope to gain by holding Dolly Lamoureux."

"Wait a minute, now," I said. "Did Dolly say she got a note that George was in the hospital and that she should come back from her picnic?"

"Yes, that's it. How'd you know?"

"Tell you later. For now, let's see about getting her out. Where's the jail?"

"Right now, she's upstairs. That horse's ass Sarge is talking to her."

"I'll see you later." I crept up to Government House on my crutches, carefully mounting eighteen steps while trying not to wiggle my gimpy knee, shifting a quarter turn to the right, and hobbling up another ten to the second landing. I raised a hand to knock on the door. I walked in instead, without knocking. I ignored Dolly Lamoureux and walked over to Sarge. "Sarge," I said, "you're making a terrible mistake. And think what that can do to tourism. You shouldn't be arresting tourists like this."

Sarge glared. "Mrs. Lamoureux is not under arrest. I am simply questioning her about the accident. In fact, we are just about to an end, and if you will kindly wait outside, the lady will be free to join you in a minute." His voice was molded gelatin in a gale, sweet and bland, but trembling furiously.

I looked at her. "Please go," she said. "I'll be all right."

"I'll be outside." I waited maybe ten minutes, and the door opened. A white-faced, tear-streaked Dolly Lamoureux emerged, and nearly collapsed into my arms.

"Oh, by God," she said. "You know that awful man kept me an extra ten minutes just to let you know who was boss. He practically told me so! But it's true. He's not concerned about me or about Elizabeth Olds or anything except his tourist trade. Even if the poor woman had been found with a rope knotted around her neck he would have called it an accident, and questioning me was only the idiot's way of making everything look legal. He *wants* me innocent and off his miserable island, and oh, believe me, I've never wanted anything so much myself in my life!" She burst into tears, and fell heavily against me for support.

I patted her shoulder into a state resembling calm, and bit by bit got the story. A hotel maid had brought a note that her husband was in the hospital and that she was needed immediately. I asked her for it. She didn't have it. She had crumpled it and let it drop. She thought the maid had picked it up again, but she wasn't sure. She left Elizabeth Olds without even thinking about it, and ran back to the town. And of course there was nothing wrong with George.

"Do you remember what the note said? I mean the exact words?"

She screwed up her face and thought. With her eyes shut, she said, "Yes, I can see it in my mind. I think I'll see it forever. It said, 'Your husband is very ill. He is in hospital. Come at once.'" She opened her eyes. "That was it."

"Well," I said, trying to sound as if that meant something to me. "Aha," I added knowingly. "Let's go downstairs. Mr. Lamoureux is half crazy with worry. Just tell me one thing first: which maid brought you that note?"

She told me it was June, the "sort of yellow-skinned one." I made a mental note to talk to the sort of yellow-skinned one.

I saw the happy couple into each other's arms in the lobby, the two of them wailing like modified wolves. The Hollands were standing by, Randolph with his hands in his pockets looking as if he would have preferred being elsewhere, and

Loretta looking cool and distant as if she were in fact elsewhere, somewhere where the howling was from cats instead of wolves.

I backed off. I had done enough. I joined Jane, Ken Tillson, and the lovely Carlla at the other side of the lobby, and we watched the proceedings from a civilized distance.

Carlla was sunburned. "Hey," I said, "what's with you, sweetheart, too much outdoors?"

"Oh, God," Carlla snarled. "This creep," she said, jerking her head toward Kenny, "took me out in a sailboat today. We got back a while ago and found this mess here. He never told me he couldn't sail a toy boat in a bath tub! We couldn't get the stupid boat into the harbor, and the sun was awful, and listen, Tillson, listen to me good; if I start peeling I won't be able to model a stinking Mother Hubbard, much less a two-piece bathing suit, and I'll have your ass, you hear? On toast!"

"Whole wheat or white?" Kenny asked.

"Don't be so funny. As it is, we'd better shoot the next scenes in soft focus, with me in lots of flowing organdy, you shit!"

"Hey, will you two cut it out!" I said. "We've got enough trouble around here without you yapping."

"Yeah," Carlla said, looking at the group across the room. "You know," she added, "everybody's weeping and sobbing, but I'll bet you none of it is for Elizabeth Olds, even if this ought to be her party. I guess it doesn't matter, though. Old Lizzie didn't approve of life, so she shouldn't have minded cutting out too much."

"Oh, come on, Carlla," Jane said. "The woman was alive, after all. Don't tell me she brought it on herself or anything like that."

"That's not what I mean," Carlla said, "but look at the difference with her husband. You know what Henry said to me the last time I spoke to the old sweetie? He said that he used to be afraid of getting old, but now that he was there it was like going into a health food restaurant: more fun than he thought it would be, even though if he had any choice he'd just as soon live without it. Isn't that kicky?

"And he told me the old battle-ax was the other way around; when she got old she didn't want to have fun, but just wanted to see that nobody else had any fun either. That's why he stuck it to her that he was going to sell out to Holland and retire, so Lizzie would get the idea that her time for dumping on the world was about over. He didn't mean it, of course, but he liked to see her sweat."

"Well, if that's fun," I said, "I'd hate to have been around when he wasn't feeling funny."

"Yeah?" Carlla returned, "you should be only half so funny as Henry Olds. One time when he was feeling sorry for himself and kept going on about how he used to be such a sexpot and now here he was with me and all he could do was talk and he was glad he was going to die soon and all that sort of garbage, I told him to cut it out. I said after he died he could have a big marble tombstone and he could carve on it STIFF AT LAST. You know what he said after he stopped laughing? He said hell, no, that'd just get Lizzie to jumping into the box with him, that's what he said."

"Okay," I said, "that's pretty funny, but only in a ghoulish way. What do you think, Kenny?"

"Huh?" Ken said. "I'm sorry. I wasn't listening. I was looking at Loretta there. What the hell do you think of that?"

Loretta Holland had an arm around the sobbing Dolly Lamoureux, and was muttering trenchant and un-Loretta-like inanities of comfort, like "there, there, there, there," and "there now, there now," following each syllable with a comforting pat on the back.

"That *can't* be my Loretta! Much as I love the girl, I've got to say that she's much too wrapped up in herself to go around dispensing solace. Too middle-class, I should have thought." Ken shifted gears into the bitch mode and drawled on. "No, darling, you can usually count on Loretta to look on other people's troubles as imaginary, and their complaints as putting on airs. If she's got an arm around that blubberpuss, there's some kind of nourishment in it for her, and it ain't the milk of human kindness."

"You can say that again," Carlla muttered.

"I'm getting out of here," I said. "I'm just a simple country boy, and you two are too much for me. You coming, Jane?"

"I'm going back to the bungalow and lie down," Jane said. "See you all later."

Jane and I headed off in opposite directions, she for the front door, and I for the rear of the lobby.

This time I didn't ask at the desk. I got into my motorized conveyance—my leg got itself overused on the crutch-supported stomp up and down those stairs—and sailed into the back quarters where the staff rooms were. I found June without any trouble, and asked her who gave her the note.

She looked sullen. "Mister, I don't know about no note. What note?"

"Didn't you go out to those two ladies at the lagoon to-day?"

"Sure I went out. I took 'em a picnic basket. Chicken and some salad and fruit and a jug of coffee, but no note. You go ask in the kitchen, you don't believe me."

"You know that one of those ladies says you brought her a note and that after she read it, you picked it off the ground and took it with you."

"I don't care what she say. She a crazy lady, mister, shoutin' and screamin' like everything." She hefted a mop that was leaning against the wall. "I got work to do, mister. I got no time for talk. You excuse me, okay?"

Back in the cottage Jane and I talked it over. "Just for the hell of it," I said, "let's ask ourselves why Dolly Lamoureux would lie. The simplest explanation is that the Olds woman accidentally fell into the lagoon, or maybe even committed suicide—"

"I doubt that," Jane said. "Not that tough old bird."

"—and Dolly panicked. Figured she'd get blamed some-how. So she makes up this crazy story, figuring nobody can blame her for anything if she wasn't there when it happened. Whatever it was that happened."

"But if there was a note," Jane asked, "why would the maid lie about it?"

"She'd only lie if someone told her to."

"Sarge?"

I nodded. "Sarge."

"But why?"

"I was just about to ask you that," I said.

"Sarge's main concern is to keep things cool down here," Jane said. "If there had been a note, that would mean someone was up to something very involved. Sarge wouldn't like that one bit unless he was in on it. Bad for tourism. But the other way, all he's got is one very demented, hysterical woman afraid someone will blame her for what was almost certainly a fatal accident."

"Which do you think is more likely?"

"If you want the truth, neither one. Too many moving parts in all these explanations to get anywhere talking like this. That's how I feel about it, anyway."

"Me too. I'll buy the idea that Sarge could be in it up to his teeth," I said, "but it's too complicated. Know what I think? I think we should get the hell out of this tropical splendor. My leg is okay now, and better to lose a leg than your ass, the way I feel about it. Both our asses."

"First sensible idea either of us has had yet."

That's what we did. It's true I'm a coward, but on the other hand I do have a certain sense of social responsibility, so as soon as we had arranged to catch the flight the next afternoon, I got through by phone to Henry Olds's nephew and told him, though using gentler terms, that there'd be a large refrigerated package arriving by air, C.O.D., in a day or so, and he'd be well-advised to prepare himself in advance.

About twenty minutes after I had made the flight arrangements, a policeman showed up at the door. I could tell he was a cop because he wore a T-shirt that read "Vancouver World's Fair, 1986," needed a shave, and wore a gun belt with a Mars bar, open, tucked in it. He also carried an impressive billy which looked as if it had been carved out of a single palm tree, and which he kept rapping into the palm of his hand.

"Sarge wanna see you," he said. "Now."

I weighed the alternatives, and decided they were nonexistent. "Okay," I said, "coming. Jane, if I'm not back in an hour—swim," I added with much more bravado than I felt.

Government House was beginning to feel like my home away from home. This time there were no chairs borrowed from the lobby. Sarge sat, which at least allowed me to learn whether he kept his belly above the desk or below it. (Neither: the desk creased it mid-ship.)

"Mr. Franklin," he said.

"That's me," I returned. "Is there anything else?"

"It is my unpleasant duty to inform you that you are no longer welcome on our island. You are upsetting our citizens, you accuse them of lying because they will not go along with these poppycock stories about secret notes and other similar nonsense. The court has granted a writ ordering your deportation. You will leave on the plane tomorrow afternoon. That is all. Do you have any questions?"

He knew perfectly well I had already made reservations to leave, but he needed the last word. Like You-can't-fire-me-I-quit. "But why?" I asked. "What have I done? Just ask a girl a few questions?" I tried to sound aggrieved, which I wasn't, but I thought I might learn something by being heartbroken.

"I think you know. All of you, you treat us like idiots. Your Mrs. Lamoureux lets her companion drown, or perhaps she even drowns her herself, and tries to make mischief to save her own precious hide. We cannot afford your games, Mr. Franklin! We live on tourism, as you very well know. And the more upset you people cause with your stupid games, the more my people starve. We cannot afford your behavior. Now do you understand? Leave us, Mr. Franklin, and I shall inform your Department of State that you shall never be allowed back in San Sebo unless reparations are forthcoming. Is that clear? Now go." He turned his head down to his desk, as if to fiddle with his papers now that I had been dismissed. The effect was a good one, being perhaps only slightly marred by the lack of any papers for him to fiddle with. Maybe I was wrong; maybe he was studying his stomach to see if it had been sufficiently awake to admire him playing Trash the Tourist.

Back with Jane again, I heaved a sigh.

"What happened?" she asked. "What's wrong?"

"Nothing," I replied. "Not a thing. Sarge just wanted to confirm our reservations. And very thoughtful of him it was."

"Good. But I'm not going to trust that son of a bitch to carry my bags. Let's go enjoy our last few hours on the beach, and store up memories of a perfect vacation. Like in the travel folders. Even if the sun is getting low."

I agreed. "Like in the travel folders."

We trotted, Jane like a beauty queen and I like a one-legged pirate without portfolio, down to the beach where we sagged onto the sand. We did little talking.

A large sailboat left the harbor and passed directly in front of us. A roundish little lady was standing in the prow and next to her an average size man had a protective arm around her. I waved. "The Lamoureuxs," I said to Jane. "Hail and farewell."

"Good," Jane said sleepily. "I feel better already."

Fifteen minutes later a small private jet buzzed overhead. "Hallelujah," I sighed. "I hope it's the Hollands."

"Keep talking. I'm feeling even better. Let me know if Sarge takes off too. Out to sea in a cement overcoat."

"That happens, we'll stay on a couple of days."

Jane didn't answer. I looked over. She was asleep.

Later I woke her and we went back to the cottage, dressed, and went to dinner. We ate with almost no conversation, and it was lovely. It's marvelous how relaxed a place can get to be once your colleagues have left and taken their friendship with them. I was half asleep with the joy of it all.

On second thought, maybe I was completely asleep. And maybe I never woke Jane at all. And at the time, we both liked it that way, no maybe about it.

We crawled into bed early, rather than be mistaken for the walking dead by Sarge's gendarmerie.

TWELVE

I slept until nearly ten the next morning. Jane was already up and sitting on the front steps reading a book and contemplating the fallen mango, which had continued apace on its course toward ultimate corruption. "Morning, love," I said. "Let's eat, maybe?"

"I thought you'd never ask."

As we started down the path, I saw little Andy sitting patiently. He held a stack of perhaps a dozen sheets of paper and he was sketching our bungalow. "Oh, Lord," I said, "Andy. I forgot all about you being here this morning. Have you been waiting long?"

He gave us his bashful smile. "No, it's all right. Doc got me paper from his friend at the hospital last night. So while I wait for you here I can draw your house."

"Come here, Andy, and let me see," Jane said. "I'm Mrs. Franklin, and I'm happy to meet you."

Andy instantly backed off and looked at me for reassurance. "It's okay, Andy," I said. "Let Mrs. Franklin see what you've been drawing." The boy came over and with a tentative smile handed over his sketch.

Jane looked at it. "Why, that's beautiful, son!" she said. "I'd like to buy that from you. As a remembrance of our trip to San Sebo. All right?"

"No," the boy said. "It's not finished. My momma don't like me to sell not good pictures." He put his hand out and stood his ground until Jane put the paper back into his grasp. The boy looked at me, his eyebrows raised. "You say you give me some paper today?" We could scarcely hear him speak, and he sounded as if prepared for total rejection, as if he had learned in the past that the average tourist was an unreliable source of anything but promises.

"Oh, sure, Andy. I'll get your paper." I had completely forgotten, of course. "Jane, my leg is a little hurtish. Would you go over to the big house and cop a slew of paper from the writing desk off the lobby?"

Jane left. I took Andy back to the steps of the cottage, where we both sat. "How's your momma and Doc?"

"They fine. Momma got this bad ache in the arm she get sometimes, but Doc got good medicine."

"Doc got medicine?" I asked.

The boy looked at me with the same friendly scorn that Jane's son Billy laid on me when I displayed a typical grown-up lack of common sense. "Sure he got medicine. Doc's a doctor, isn't he?"

I laughed at the funny little fellow; sometimes that clear logic of childhood can lead to some fairly foolish conclusions. Or so I thought. "Let's see the rest of those pictures you've got there, Andy."

He handed over the papers. Besides the one of the bungalow Jane and I were in, there were drawings of the other bungalows and the beach and trees in the area. As with the pictures I had seen before, these were all on the backs of sheets used by somebody for some other purpose and in some other place. "My, these are good," I said. "You must have been waiting for me a long time."

You can't fool a kid, unless you're better than I am. He saw through my feeble ploy. "Not long enough to finish. I take them now, okay?" He gently but firmly disengaged his masterpieces from my hot and greedy fingers.

Jane came back. "Here we are," she said. "Here's your paper, Andy. Make pretty pictures, you hear."

"Thank you," the boy said in his shy voice again. He reached for the paper, smiled happily, and sped off without another word. I think he felt about being with Jane and me the way we felt about being with the board of directors of Finch, Rowan, & Hyde.

We started down the path toward the main house to see about breakfast, when Andy came charging back. "Mister! Lady!" he called. "I almost forgot. Doc, he say he got something he want to show you, you come over now."

"What is it, son? What's Doc got to show us?"

"I dunno, but Doc say come over."

I looked at my watch. "Okay, Andy, just as soon as we get something to eat, I'll be right over. Tell Doc I'll be there in a little while, okay?"

"Okay. I tell him." The boy turned and scooted off again. Jane and I continued on toward breakfast.

Half an hour later I wound my weary way, encrutched for what I intended to be the last time, to my island friend's cottage. I found Juleen sitting in a canvas chair in front, her legs drawn up, huddled into herself, hiding from the world, while Andy was standing a few feet away, as if afraid to get any closer to his mother. His sheaf of papers was under his arm, and his hands were clenched into frightened fists that he held in front of him, ready to repel the world.

Juleen turned her face away. "You go 'way, man," she said, "you go 'way. Doc isn't here. Please go."

"Where is Doc? What's wrong, Juleen?"

She looked up at me. "He's gone. They took him away. While Andy was over at your bungalow to get paper."

"Who? Who took him away?"

"The police is who. The police, Sarge, I don't know. Look at the house, just look!" She waved an arm toward the door.

I went over and peered in. My eyes took a moment to adjust to the dark interior, and then I saw. The place was in chaos. The boxes that held their few possessions were overturned, the beds were pulled apart, whatever could have been overturned or opened was overturned and opened, the shabby straw rug was shoved to one side, and the photographs that had been on the wall had been ripped from their frames and cast aside.

"The men, they took all my pictures," Andy said in a quiet voice.

"And they stole my nice copper pot that Doc brought me from the States when he come back," Juleen added. "And my momma's cushions. Anything good we got, they took, the men. Anything they or their women could use. My new dress."

"Okay, but what about Doc? Did they say where they were taking him? When he's coming back?"

Juleen hauled herself out of the chair and put her hands on her hips. She looked at me as she would have looked at a troublesome fool. She shook her head. "Man," she said, "Doc ain't never coming back. Never. Ever since Sarge threw him out of the hospital we knew this was coming some day. Once those police of his drag a man off you don't ever expect to see him again. Maybe some men, but not Doc. Sarge, he hates Doc, ever since—" Her voice trailed off.

"Ever since what, Juleen? You can tell me," I urged.

"Well, ever since the time when Doc was still at the hospital and he said all those folk who were working at the hotel they had that liver sickness that they got from the bad clams and things."

"Hepatitis?"

"That's the one. And Sarge said no tourists would come if anybody knew and Doc said that that was why we had to let people know and Sarge just threw him out of his job and—"

"Wait a minute," I interrupted. "You mean that Doc was a doctor at the hospital?"

"'Course he was a doctor. That's why we call him Doc. What you think?" Her patience snapped. "Oh, hell, man, what difference does it make! Doc's gone. The police left some stuff Doc wanted you to have, 'cause it just junk and those thieves they couldn't use it." She waved a hand vaguely toward some rubble. "Take it, mister, take it with you, you want it, and leave little Andy and me. We got to stay here, and you ain't doing us no good a-tall being here. Please, mister, you want it, you take it." She turned away.

"All right, Juleen. I'm sorry. Andy," I said, "show me what Doc wanted me to have." I held out my hand and the boy led me over to one side.

"This stuff here," he said. "Junk."

"Just that?" I asked in surprise.

Juleen had had enough. "Mister, how the hell do I know? If Doc had something else for you, I don't know. Please, take it and go. Please, mister."

There were two paper sacks, torn, that had once contained sugar. I turned them both over several times, and inspected the insides as well as the outsides, looking for a message or clue of some kind. I failed to find it. And there was a knitting needle, not particularly clean, but covered with the dirt of having lain outside for a day or two instead of in somebody's knitting bag. I assumed that it belonged to Elizabeth Olds, but why Doc wanted me to have it I had no idea.

I gathered up these prizes and prepared to leave. "Juleen," I said, "I'm sorry. This card has my address on it. If I can ever help you, please write me."

She took the card from my hand and relented a bit. "That's all right. Look," she added, "I can tell you maybe something. Those paper bags. Doc got them over where the planes come in. He told me that much, but I don't know nothing else. And I don't know where that needle come from."

I was pretty sure the needle came from Mrs. Olds's things on the shore of the lagoon, but what that might have signified eluded me. "Well, thank you, Juleen. I wish there was something I could do." She didn't answer, so I quietly started walking away.

A little way down the beach, I called softly to the boy, "Andy, come here a minute, will you?" He came toward me, but very slowly. "Here," I said, giving him what I had in my pocket, which came to a little over thirty dollars. "After I'm away from here, you give this to your momma, okay?"

He nodded solemnly, and I left him standing alone, the ocean gently lapping at his toes, his thoughtful eyes glued on me in doubt and wonder, looking frail and vulnerable against a background of sand and swaying coconut palms.

Back in the room, I tucked the sugar sacks and the knitting needle into my bag, my sole sourvenirs of a sojourn that was all too unforgettable, but not in the sense that travel agents have in mind when they compose their deathless prose.

"What in God's name do you want that garbage for?" Jane asked.

"I don't know," I said. "I just have the feeling it may mean something. Anyway, Doc thought so, so what the hell. I can always throw it out."

"You mean *I* can always throw it out. If it was up to you, you'd still have the ticket stubs for the '78 World Series in your sock drawer."

"Gee whiz! So it was you threw them out. Only the other day I was wondering where they got to. I'll be damned."

"Keep it up, Buster, and you will be."

I know when to knock it off with Jane, so I closed my bag and my mouth simultaneously until it was time to call for transportation to the airport.

The feeder airline that was to take us to San Juan lifted off on time, and my heart took wing in harmony with it. At San Juan we transferred to United. I hobbled over to an attendant at the lineup, exaggerating my condition perhaps a shade dramatically.

"What are you trying to do," Jane asked, "look like one of our glorious war dead?"

"You'll find out," I told her.

I explained to the attendant that I couldn't wait on line because of an injury to my leg, and that I'd like to be met with a wheelchair at Kennedy in New York. She told me she'd take care of it, but to make doubly certain I should repeat my request for the wheelchair to the on-board flight attendant, and would I like an aisle seat so that I could stretch my leg out, and she'd be delighted to take care of it for me. The young lady was as abnormally efficient as she was pretty, which was very.

"Oh, thank you," I said, "that'd be great. And I guess you can take care of my wife's seat at the same time?"

The young lady and I smiled at each other, and as she left to do the little errands on our behalf, I said to Jane, "Isn't she a doll? And so helpful!"

"Yeah. And I'm glad she got you an aisle seat, because if you were next to the window I might just push you out the effing plane, you smartassed bastard!"

"What did I do now?"

"I'll tell you all about it on the plane." She did, too. Some women can't bear it when other women find their husbands attractive.

When we got to Kennedy I hopped into the waiting wheelchair, and we tooled down the endless corridors to collect the luggage. Then we rolled outside to the endless taxi line. "Now you'll see," I whispered.

The porter wheeled me to the front of the line and spoke to the dispatcher, who nodded briskly, and put me in the next cab. I larded both gentlemen with silver and struggled aboard. As I did so I heard cries of "What the hell's going on!" and "I was here ahead of that guy," and "Some people got a lot of moxie," and "What kind of bull do you call that?" and a few even more choice expressions of endearment.

I settled back and explained. "See? And ain't it awful how terrible people in Noo Yawk can be to a poor cripple?"

The driver overheard me and said, "You folks visiting for the first time?"

Hoping to discourage conversation, I answered with a terse, "That's right. And we're very tired."

"Like me to show you around a little?"

"Not today. We're too worn out. Just take us to the address I gave you, okay?"

"Okay, Mac."

We rode in silence for a spell, and both Jane and I fell into a daze just short of sleep. I looked up at one point, however, in time to see the cab cutting off the Triboro Bridge to the Bronx instead of heading for the Manhattan exit. "Gee whiz," I exclaimed, "I guess they've moved the East Eighties way up north, huh, driver? Or were you figuring on dumping us in the Bronx Zoo with the rest of the sheep?"

"Oh, gee, I guess I took the wrong turn. Sorry 'bout that, Mac."

"Yeah, I bet."

Eventually, we got home. I gave the driver precisely the amount indicated on the meter. "Where's the tip, Mac?" he asked.

"It's in there," I explained. "Take it out of the detour to the Bronx," I explained. "Mac."

He zoomed off, leaving an inch of his employer's rubber steaming and stinking on the street as the tires squealed in an effort to keep up with the rest of the cab.

"I hate New York," I said to Jane. "I hate San Sebo."

"No more than me," Jane said.

"If we ever get to live up there on the orchard, I'm never going further than I can lob an apple."

Jane looked critically at my raddled frame, at the limp I was sporting even without the exaggeration, and at my blood-shot eyes. "Better make it no further than you can lob a watermelon, sweetie."

I put my arm around her and we dragged into the lobby to find a handyman to get our luggage up to the apartment, where we planned on sinking instantly into drink and other forms of degradation.

THIRTEEN

Time progressed. I tried passing myself off as an office hero by limping pathetically, but nobody bought it. In fact, nobody even noticed, except for one art director who hates me, and what he said was, "What's the matter with you, dear boy? Trip over a research report?" He placed an index finger along his cheek and looked at me quizzically, lips pursed. "Catch a heel in your hem, did you?"

"No," I snarled sweetly, "I caught it in a pink slip. I think it belonged to an art director."

The thing is that researchers and artists in ad agencies are a bit less than totally fond of each other. The artists are convinced that researchers want only to destroy their sacred creativity by telling them how to do their jobs, while in fact researchers are only trying to point out that if you think you're putting across the idea of quality in a premium beer with an endorsement from the Duchess of Parma, you're wrong. There'd be a consumer study to show that among truck drivers who are asked about the ad, 81 percent would agree "I think it stinks," 17 percent would say it "sounds like some kind of grated cheese," and the rest would decide that "the old broad looks like a lousy lay."

Three days later, when my tan was almost completely faded, one of the research crew said, "Didn't get much sun down there, did you?"

So I stopped thinking about San Sebo.

And a few days after that, a copywriter caught me in the hall. "Hey," he said, "I thought you were going off to some Caribbean resort. St. Martin's or something. What're you doing here?"

"Just fucking around for a living, like everybody else. And I wish I didn't have to." Oh, how I wished it.

It was all in the past, and I forgot about it, except for those few minutes of the day after going to bed and closing my eyes and waiting for sleep. That's when it nagged at me. But there was nothing I could do and nothing I should do, though there would have been something I would do, if only I could have figured out what it might have been. There may or may not have been a couple of murders, a friendly old man and a bartender had vanished, possibly forever, and it wasn't right. It simply wasn't right.

Sometimes I think what set me off was that vile Sunday afternoon party Jane and I had to go to at her kid brother's house. Her brother's a decent enough type, and so's his wife, if being pleasantly bored is your bag, and they had a party for all the couples in their neighborhood with babies up to about two years old. They figured, as they frequently did, that Jane and I should be exposed to the good life and that maybe we'd settle down and breed like nice people, especially since our breeding years were rapidly tobogganing to a close.

There we were. There were perhaps a dozen couples in the room, each with a kid in a carriage or a stroller or a crib or plopped into a pen, while everybody talked formulas and poundage. (In some cases ounceage.) The major excitement bubbled up at fifteen-minute intervals when the mommies would lift their heads, crane their lovely necks and, nostrils twitching, sniff the air like lionesses on guard against some dimly sensed danger. One or another would rise and trot from carriage to stroller to crib to pen until she could announce, "It's your Bobby, Diane." Diane would get up, take Bobby into the next room, change his diapers, and cart him back again, and the conversation would pick up where it had broken off, at either formulas or poundage. Then it would be sniff time again for Helen's Shirley or Ruth's Norman, or possibly for some future Mrs. Borden's Lizzie, though that may have been asking too much. And the minutes sped like hours.

We finally excused ourselves. "I need something more thrilling in my life," I complained to Jane in the car. "Loaded guns, maybe, but no more loaded diapers."

"You think I liked it?"

"It's your brother, not mine."

"If your parents were smart enough not to try for something else after you were born, don't you natter at me, Everett Franklin."

"Okay, okay. But I need some excitement. I've got to lift these rheumy eyes to something higher than a baby's crotch."

It could just be coincidence, but it wasn't long after that numbing episode that I began to get some ideas.

Of course, George Lamoureux's trip to New York might also have had something to do with it.

Ed Jorgensen brought him into my office. "Got a surprise visitor for you, Ev. Look who's here, fresh from the heartland of America."

"Well, George Lamoureux!" I said. "This *is* a surprise. Dolly with you?"

"No, I'm here on a fast business trip and thought I'd drop in. Got into town yesterday, going back tomorrow. Besides," he said with a laugh, while heaving himself into a chair,

"Dolly says the shopping's better in Tulsa than in New York anyway."

As I recalled the lady's ample bod, I thought he was probably right; flour sacks are likely to be a better buy nearer to the point of origin. And I have nothing against spending money wisely.

Big Ed broke in. "Well, good to see you, George," he said, clapping the visitor on the back. "I'll leave you in Ev's good hands here and get back to my desk. See you at the next board meeting, if not before."

"Right. See you at Pebble Beach, then. On the links, right?"

Jorgensen agreed, laughed, and left, the rat.

I wondered if I was going to get any work done, but I knew my duty to the board of directors. "Care for some coffee, George? Or would you like to go down for something stronger?"

"No, no, nothing at all. I dropped in to say hello. And good-bye, that's all."

I tried not to breathe a sigh of relief. "That's too bad. How're things going with you?" I asked, meaning, are you out on your duff, or is your bank still managing to hold on.

"Couldn't be better." He hesitated. "Shucks, I guess you know the story. It could be better, but a couple of months ago I thought it was going to be a helluva lot worse. Anyway, we're hanging on, and if Congress starts listening to the voters, they'll be helping the farmers out, and if they help the farmers, they'll be helping us. I hate to say it," and his voice dropped to a whisper, "but thank God Ronald Reagan will be out of the White House soon. I mean, he's a wonderful man and I voted for him twice, but what the hell, you can't ignore the farm crisis, can you?"

"I guess not."

"Anyway, you know that Lizzie Olds was going to send us down the tube as if we were responsible for what happened to old Henry, and she meant it too. But thank the Lord—I mean, I'm sorry about her and all that, but I guess you know the nephew inherited, Allie Biedermeier, and he's been very good about things. Very reasonable. Staying with us. Figures we all got to stick together in these times. So we're going to make it just fine."

"Glad to hear it."

He laughed. "You know, for a while back there, I was wondering if Dolly really did do it, if she pushed that old—well, you know what I mean. Dolly's a wonderful gal, and I think she'd do anything for the two of us. To protect us, I mean. A real Christian lady, my Dolly is, and that's the truth. You know I'm only kidding about her doing anything like that to another human being, but, gosh almighty! She had me wondering myself for a couple of split seconds." He laughed again, most unconvincingly.

"Well, it's over now," I said soothingly, "and it looks like it was an accident. Sad, unfortunate, but life has to go on." I figured I just passed Hypocrisy 101 with honors.

"You said a mouthful there, Ev, a mouthful."

We bowed our several heads in respectful memory of Henry and Elizabeth Olds.

"Okay, then, friend," Lamoureux said, "I won't take up any more of your time. Give my regards to your lovely bride, and tell her I hope I'll see the both of you out at Pebble Beach. Okay?"

"Okay it is," I returned heartily, "and you tell Dolly I was asking after her too, you hear?" (Land sakes alive!)

We both stood, everybody clapped everybody else on the back, and George Lamoureux left me alone, bemused, and bewildered. What kind of a character puts on a shit-kicking country boy act like that and expects anybody over twelve to believe it? Who, while he knew damned well that something very strange had gone on in San Sebo and that it was far from certain as to what had happened, would bat his innocent eyes and do so much to implicate his wife, while at the same time saying he knew she could never have done anything like kill another human being? Why bring it up at all?

Unless of course he knew she had done it and was trying, with a great deal of ineptitude, to express his certainty of her innocence.

Or unless he knew that somebody else killed Elizabeth Olds and was pretending that such an idea had never crossed his mind. Someone else. Someone like George Lamoureux himself? Maybe there actually was a note sent to start Dolly Lamoureux galloping away from the beach and over to the hospital. And maybe George Lamoureux wrote it.

That evening Jane and I were sitting at home watching the news on television before dinner. It was my turn in the kitchen and I had been so bored at work since we got back that I was actually planning a meal that wouldn't give us any leftovers; I'd have to start all over from the beginning the next day. What with veal scallops costing what they did, I was using turkey slices. I'd coat them with flour and sauté them fast, dumping in some Madeira at the end, et voilà, poor man's Veau à la Madère. I was waiting for Billy to say something about cheapos who used turkey instead of veal, but I was ready. It was the rotten kid's doing that I had to use safflower oil instead of butter, because like all kids these days he had lit on the evils of saturated fat and cholesterol with the same passion that his counterparts in eighteenth-century Salem, Massachusetts, had fingered Satan as the source of all the trouble in the world.

Meantime the rice was on low and the TV set on high. Billy was in the room too, earphones clapped on his head so he could listen to one of his cassettes while he watched the news and incidentally—very incidentally—make believe he was doing something with an algebra text; most likely drawing dirty pictures in the margin, if you'd have asked me. The news reached the hair-raising human interest section where they dote on humiliating some poor soul by televising his or her personal agonies to the millions. This time it was an attractive young woman in her thirties humbly posing while the camera zoomed in her bald pate, which a professorial commentator explained had been caused by illegal dumping of radioactive wastes in a pond near her home. I jumped up and turned down the sound.

"Listen," I said to Jane, "what's your opinion? You think either Henry or Elizabeth Olds was murdered? No, let me take that back. *If* they were both knocked off, who'd be your favorite candidate for killer?"

"Bonnie and Clyde," was the reply, offered without a moment's hesitation.

"Sweetheart, I know I'm being stupid, but bear with me. Do you think Dolly Lamoureux could have done it? We know she could have figured there was reason enough, what with the Oldses planning on throwing her old man into bankruptcy. Jane, don't look at me like that! Humor me, willya?"

"Okay. I'll skip over the fact that a perfectly good and respectable hospital certified the old fellow's death as the result of a heart attack. What happened to Elizabeth is a little fuzzier, I'll grant you. So." She put a set expression on her face and looked right at me. "So. Yes, Dolly is a reasonable candidate, if you must have one. She was feeding drinks to the old boy and I suppose could have slipped some poison in, though frankly I think it's silly. I mean, poisons that don't leave any traces is out of an old-fashioned mystery book. Nancy Drew. Philo Vance. And she certainly was on the scene near the time that Elizabeth died, and this story of a note calling her away because her husband was in the hospital is awfully fishy."

"Thank you," I said. "How about George Lamoureux? Could he have been the killer?"

"Well, he couldn't have poisoned any drinks, I don't think. That lets him out for Henry Olds. I suppose he could have sent a note to Dolly and once she was out of the way he might have disposed of Elizabeth. Look, Ev, if you want to play games, they both could have been the killer.

Like I said, Bonnie and Clyde. They could have worked it as a team."

"Yeah. I hadn't thought of that. What about the Hollands?"

"What about the Hollands? Okay, okay, don't get into an uproar. Yes, Loretta could've slipped something into a drink. No, Randy probably couldn't have. Yes, either one of them could have disposed of Elizabeth. But wait a minute, didn't you tell me little Andy said something about the big lady who was fighting? That would let Randolph out, unless he was in drag. And as long as you're going to play games, it'd let Carlla in, at least for killing Elizabeth. She's big, she was mad as hell, and who knows what kind of trouble the old bat was threatening her with?"

"I guess all our ladies were big, at least in little Andy's eyes. Loretta is a head taller than anybody on San Sebo, male or female, Carlla is an Amazon by any reasonable standard, and Dolly may not be very tall, but she makes up for it from side to side."

"Listen, you two," my exasperated stepson interjected, "I can't do my homework if you keep yakking, you know."

"You mean you can hear us over that cassette thing you've got your face stuck into?" I inquired pleasantly. "I can't believe it."

"That's what I mean. So don't believe it."

"And the TV picture doesn't bother you either?"

Silence from young Billy.

"Just your mother and me talking, is that it? That's what bothers you?"

Some day Billy was going to make a fine advertising executive. He was already an adept at slipping out of corners like an expert duelist and hopping on a table to confront the enemy from a better vantage point. "What bothers me is how I was in the kitchen and I see we're having turkey in veal's clothing again. How cheap can you get?"

Oh, joy. For once I was ready. "Veal scallops are eight bucks a pound at the supermarket. God knows what a butcher shop would charge. You know I wouldn't deny my family anything. But to take eight-buck-a-pound meat and dump it into safflower oil when it's whimpering for butter? No sir, young man. You don't want butter, okay, but you're lucky to get turkey. Tomorrow maybe I'll whip up a nice rare grilled tofuburger for you."

"Very funny. Go ahead, get yourself a case of the galloping cholesterols. See if I care."

"I just might at that."

"Stop it, you two," Jane commanded.

We stopped. Maybe I didn't win, but I held my own, which in this house is pretty damn good for a rapidly aging joker in the declining years.

□

FOURTEEN

□

Wheels kept spinning, but only in my head. With no certainty that any crimes had been committed, I nevertheless had a number of potential murderers and murderesses to choose among. The only progress I made was to consider one of them more seriously and then to drop her altogether.

It began with meeting Kenny Tillson in the executive dining room one day. "Sit here, sonny," a familiar voice urged as I entered with Jane for a bite of lunch, and there was Ken, his eyebrows waggling under his wig in friendly greeting.

"A pleasure," Jane said, "but no business talk, okay? We usually go out for lunch to get away from office talk, but not with the rain coming down this way."

"Agreed," Ken said. "The only good thing about office talk at table is that it spoils the appetite." He slapped a couple of his chins with the back of his hand to demonstrate his problem. "So how goes it with you two since San Whatsis?"

"Don't mention that place while we're eating," I urged. "Unless you want to tell me it's been offed by a major hurricane."

"Listen, the only major hurricane I know about down there is Karlla, and she's back in the city now."

"Carlla?"

"It's Karlla now, sweeties, with a capital K."

"The astrologer again?"

"Not quite. She's gotten jittery about the old career, the poor child, and she's bouncing around in seven directions at once, deciding that this or that or the other thing is what she needs now. Or else, judging from the storm she's kicking up, maybe it's a rehearsal for menopause. Male menopause, I think." He shook his head. "She's being awfully macho these days, you know. Snarling, snapping, roaring, and my dear, *much* chest beating. Simply awful."

"Why, for heaven's sake?"

"Who the hell knows? As far as I can figure, that old biddy, the one the fish was foolish enough to munch on—and my! but that must have been one bilious barracuda after dindin— really got to her."

Jane interrupted. "Kenny, you really are one tasteless son of a bitch, aren't you."

"Of course, darling. Recognition at last, and about time. No point in being a hypocrite about it, is there." He smiled appreciatively at Jane. "Anyway, that bearded nanny goat lit into Karlla like a laser beam. Told her she had called her lawyer to start a suit, that Karlla had seduced—hah!—her husband away from her, that she was going to get back all those crown jewels that belonged to her if she had to take it to the Supreme Court or something. And so on. I told our girl to forget it, but after the unfoooortunate demise"—he smiled at Jane wickedly—"she just fell apart. Some jerk of a therapist back here in town told her it was guilt feelings on her part, that she wanted the Olds woman dead and now she was feeling responsible. And wouldn't you know it, that only gave her the excuse to act up in the most tiresome way and go all fine nerve endings on everybody, and God but I wish some models had more brain but I suppose you can't ask for everything. Or sometimes I think for anything."

He drew an enormous breath at the end of that and subsided into an attack on a baked potato drowning in sour cream, ruined appetite or no.

I, on the other hand, put my fork down and trembled like a pointer about to flush out the quail. "Ken," I said, "tell me something. What with it sounding like Karlla's had what we used to call a nervous breakdown before they invented guilt feelings, do you think she maybe could have got into a fight with the old girl? I mean, even without meaning to, she's a pretty hefty chick and she could've walloped her too hard, maybe?"

"Oh, come off it, Franklin. You think too much."

"Yeah. That's what Jane says too."

"No I don't," Jane said. "I say you don't think at all, dummy."

"Besides," Kenny mumbled through a mouthful of potato, "how could she? We were out on that boat when the old girl got hers. Don't you remember? Karlla and that sunburn she was blaming me for? So you can drop that idea. And you'd better. I tell Karlla and she'd belt you so hard your teeth would be chewing on your liver."

I brightened. "Hey, you know? You're right! Karlla couldn't have been anywhere around Elizabeth Olds that day."

"That's what I said. You deaf, Franklin?"

"He's not deaf," Jane explained, "just dotty. And you've made him very happy, Ken. You've eliminated one suspect from guilt for a murder that wasn't even committed."

Ken smiled at Jane. "Sweetheart, it's your husband ought to be committed, if you want to know."

Jane smiled back; the two of them thought they were funny as all get out. But I didn't care. I figured I had made progress. Ten minutes ago I had five murder suspects, and now I was down to four. The fact that I might not have any murders to suspect them of was a mere technicality. Maybe I could get to that after I had narrowed the list down to one murderer. Maybe it'd be easier then.

Listen, I knew perfectly well while I was reasoning this way that it didn't make much sense, but when you're out on a limb with a power saw cutting yourself off and you can't figure out how to stop the thing, the only course open is to pretend that that's the way you want it. Maybe it wasn't precisely the way I wanted it, but we can't always have everything the way we want it in this world, can we? Oh, hell, let's change the subject.

FIFTEEN

Perversely enough, it was when I had to get my mind focussed on my job for a change and quit the fruitless brooding that I finally got a lead on what had happened, or might have happened, on San Sebo. It was when the visiting Englishman from our London affiliate, my counterpart at Balcomb and Balcomb, Ltd., turned up to discuss plans for heavying up on advertising in Britain for the increased imports from this country that we were anticipating as a result of the weaker dollar.

I wasn't particularly looking forward to Ned Hertwood's arrival, because it had been our experience at Finch, etc., that whatever remained of the old style Englishman that many people thought had disappeared with the dissolution of the Empire, had taken its final stand in Balcomb and Balcomb, Ltd. That noble institution was stocked with gents who were fervent believers in the equality of man except as it applied to Englishmen not personally known to them, and to all Americans, whether personally known or not. Their noses were generally long and horsey, and were not used for breathing; they served instead as straight edges for looking down when the rest of the world was so misguided as to assert its presence.

In fact, we worked on the theory that if the English pronounced Wymondham as Windum, and Leicester as Lester, then we had the right to refer to Balcomb and Balcomb as Bum and Bum. Or Bums, Limited.

But Ned Hertwood, poor fellow, was okay, and when on stepping off the plane and walking out the terminal door expecting traffic to approach from the right he was smitten by a New York cab, I was genuinely sorry. They took him to Jamaica Hospital for an overnight stay. "I expect being in hospital," he said ruefully, "will cut down on my expenses, assuming my insurance will cover it. But there's no other virtue to this that I can see. Oh, damn it all, I was looking forward so to greedy portions of American food and all I've got to start with is porridge even lumpier than I can get back home."

"We'll fill you with all sorts of vile American goodies once we get you sprung from this place," I assured him.

"I can hardly wait."

Fortunately, the wait was short. The hospital released Ned the next morning. He spent a short time signing papers for the taxi company's insurers stating that he had sustained no broken limbs, concussions, contusions, or other grievous injuries that he had not brought with him, whether declared at customs or not. Finally he settled himself in a hotel near the office.

Late that morning he walked in on me and said, "Do you mind awfully if we get something to eat and drink before we settle down to work. Particularly drink, if you have no objection."

"That sounds splendid," I said, slipping, as I sometimes do, into British locutions when faced with the genuine article. "Any preferences?"

"Oh, I'll leave that to you, but sooner or later, since we're in New York, I've been told I should be sure to ask for hot pastrami."

"Not your first day," I said firmly. "Your stomach will disapprove. Maybe tomorrow. Whoever told you to go for the pastrami was no friend."

"It was an art director, as I recall. I don't think the poor chap meant any harm, and, well, I don't know what they're like over here, but back home art directors aren't the brightest. Well meaning, I suppose, but definitely not bright."

We were friends already. "How do you feel about account executives?" I asked.

He frowned. "I'm a trifle sorry you asked me that."

"How so?"

"It's only that I hesitate to speak ill of the dead."

We were more than friends; we were brothers. "Hey," I said, "what are you planning to do tonight, after we get done here?"

"I haven't the foggiest. Do you have any suggestions?"

"I do. I'd suggest you come home with me and Jane—that's my wife. We'll have a couple of drinks at our place; it's always nice in a strange country to get a peek inside a native hut, see how they live. Okay?"

"Perfect."

"Then we'll go out and get you that greedy plateful you were dreaming about. We'll talk about it later. Now, maybe we should go over the clients you'll be researching when their products hit the English market."

"Less perfect, but reasonable. Just one thing—after that lunch?"

We went out for a quick bite and a less quick drink, at least for Hertwood, and then back in the office I pulled over the pile of research facts and figures I had gathered in advance of his arrival. I was supposed to be teaching him, but in at least one instance he taught me. It was a car wax that one of our clients was planning to introduce in England with a big media splash.

"Really, Ev," my visitor said, "I do think the car wax media plan needs some more consideration. We'll look into it of course, but the market is very different for us back home, especially when it comes to the automotive line."

"How so?"

"I don't want to step on anybody's toes," he started.

"But you're going to. Be my guest."

"It's this way: Every car wax that has been brought over to England from the States has bombed in the past. Except one. First, you've got to remember that an automobile is a very special thing back home. Here, you take your cars for granted, and you've commonly got two or even three cars per household. With us, universal ownership is relatively new, and our cars are practically beloved family members. And a beloved family member isn't kept in good health by feeding him advertised nostrums. He gets prescriptions for his problems from the experts."

"You've lost me."

"To cut it short, the only American car polish that has ever made it in England to this date has been one that did very little advertising, and that was in a low circulation, high prestige magazine. For the rest, distribution was concentrated through the experts, the doctors, if you will, meaning garage owners and car dealers, and they were given very generous percentages for every can they sold. The experts pushed the product to the doting automobile-owning public as something their darling needed, they referred to the prestige advertising—what little there was of it—and the product sailed into space, a phenomenal success."

"You mean success through no advertising."

"Precisely."

"The less advertising the better?"

"Not quite, but almost. Yes."

I stood. "Ned, I should pull down the blinds and swear you to secrecy. If this gets out, not only do you risk a return engagement in hospital, as you English so quaintly put it, but the president of Finch, Rowan, & Hyde may be trucked in and dumped on the next bed, possibly but not necessarily before he declares war on England. I believe every word you say, and I love it, but for heaven's sake, talk it over back home and try to sprinkle a little sugar on top, will you?"

"I understand," he said sadly. "But maybe at least I can turn out some research to make a case for keeping the advertising low key. We don't want to frighten off those proud owners, do we?"

"Maybe not, but let's not scare our proud employers either, right?"

"Okay, sorry I brought it up. Viper in the corporate bosom and all such, I suppose."

(To round off that story, I'll say briefly that Hertwood's research did indeed make a strong case for a minimum of advertising and a maximum of stroking those experts in the care and feeding of the automobile in order to get the product on a roll. There were many howls from agency brass who were unable to bear the idea of passing up commissions on advertising merely to make their client a success, and they were seconded by copywriters and artists who saw the research as an assassination attempt on their sacred creativity. Consequently, Ned's work was buried and advertising weights were heavied, particularly on television. And subsequently the product was approximately as successful as horseburgers on Rodeo Drive. Requiescat, etc.)

Nothing else that afternoon so nearly caused us to founder, and except for that one traitorous episode I enjoyed the day. Finally, I looked at my watch. "Listen," I said, "we should start thinking about this evening. Would you like me to find some unattached young lady so we can make a foursome?"

"Why, yes. This is almost too much. First, native huts and now native girls. Yes, indeed. I don't suppose that rather thin girl with the long hair I saw when I came in is available? I thought she was quite attractive."

"You mean the sort of haggard one? With dark hair, dank dark hair?"

"You might describe her that way."

"Bad choice. Lesson number one: In this country, pale, thin women with long dank hair aren't fun. They worry too much, and they're likely to express liberal opinions in excess. Especially if they have mustaches. You'd spend the evening apologizing for two hundred years of British rule in India."

"Oh. Well, actually, there was an even more attractive young lady in another office, about three doors down from here, I'd say. Also dark hair, but definitely not dank."

"Pale skin? Dramatic contrast with the dark hair? Velvety eyes?"

"Exactly. An apt description, velvet eyes."

"Did she smile at you?"

"Oh, definitely."

"I don't think she'll do, anyway."

"Why ever not?"

"To begin with, that's my wife."

"Oh. That does rather put a different complexion on things, doesn't it!"

"I'm delighted you see it that way."

"Yes. For one thing, now there's the problem of getting someone for *you* to escort to dinner, isn't there?"

How could I win against that? Anyway, we went, me escorting Jane's good friend Nancy and Hertwood with my wife on his arms, if not in them, to Windows on the World, at the top of the World Trade Center, where Ned could watch night fall across Manhattan from the highest point in town and at the same time tuck away a handsome dinner. It was, I think, a successful evening. Jane was returned to me unscathed and even pleased, the inconstant trollop. And what's more, I had learned something, without realizing it, that was to help me solve the Riddle of San Sebo, as Dame Agatha might have termed it.

SIXTEEN

Ned spent another two days with me and then it was on for briefings in other parts of the Finch, etc., empire. Four or five days later he stuck his head in my door and asked, "Busy? Got a minute?"

I waved him in and into a seat. "You still here?" I inquired. "And if it's my wife that's on your mind, the answer to your question is 'No.' Now: Is there anything else, old friend?"

"As a matter of fact, there's a wife on my mind, all right, but it's my own. I'm finished here, and I wanted to thank you for your help and your hospitality—and your wife's—before I took off. Joyce is coming over from England, and we'll be joining up for a vacation in the Caribbean."

"Good. Where're you going?"

"You may not even have heard of the place. Used to be under British rule, and there's a direct plane Joyce can get from London, so we'll be in San Sebo. It's supposed to be quite pleasant. Sandy beaches, swaying palms, golf course, and the rest of it. Do you know anything about the place?"

I knew something about it, though I made a snap decision that I'd better edit what I knew, or what I thought I knew, rather than plant the suspicion in the mind of a member of our London affiliate that there was a paranoid loony running around the halls of Finch, Rowan, & Hyde. So I told Ned Hertwood about a board member suffering a fatal heart attack in San Sebo, and the subsequent demise of his distraught lady.

I did, however, suggest he look in on Juleen and little Andy, and I went so far as to make a few delicately negative observations on the state of democracy in the island republic. "And," I concluded, "they not only dragged off this elegant old man, apparently because Sarge didn't like his face, but they ransacked the poor woman's house and carried off whatever little she had that was of any value."

"Why, that's awful. Terrible."

"Oh, you won't have anything to worry about yourself. Sarge loves tourists. He'll see to it that a tourist has a good time even if he has to knock off half the locals to do it. You know, I just thought of something, telling you about the police tearing Juleen's place apart."

"Namely?"

"Well, if the police were looting for their personal fun and profit, why would they pull the pictures off the wall? That couldn't have had any value for them, not like Juleen's pots and clothing. And why would they want the kid's pictures? It doesn't figure. Except for that, everything they took was something they could use."

"Unless it was your Lord Sarge who wanted the pictures."

I shrugged. "Could be, I suppose. Anyway," I said in order to get off the mystery, "if you or your wife are at all interested, you can pick up some of this kid's drawings for yourselves. He's a real talent, and if you go for souvenirs, this beats jolly peasants made out of pink sea shells by a mile. Which gives me an idea," I said slyly, my voice all light and innocent as the dawn. "You could do me a big favor, if you would."

He nodded, and I went on. "There are a handful of pictures Jane is just dying to get hold of, and I think little Andy may still have them, because while the police were ripping off everything else, he was visiting Jane and me. There are about half a dozen or so, all sketches of the cottage Jane and I were in, or the immediate vicinity, and Jane'd love to have them. Juleen only lets the boy take small change, but see if you can get him to take a little more. They're worth it, and I'm sure they can use the cash."

Ned agreed, and insisted on paying for the pictures himself, as a return for my hospitality in New York. "I'll pop them into an envelope of some sort, if they're still in existence, and ship them off directly. And if you're ever in London—"

"You bet," I said.

He left, and I watched him walk toward the elevators, stopping only to look in on Jane's office and bid her a fond farewell. His visit had been a complete success, as far as I could judge, for Ned himself, Jane and me, for Finch, Rowan, & Hyde and Balcomb and Balcomb, and possibly for retribution and for justice, whatever the latter may be.

Of course, I'm never allowed to walk on air for very long without being shot down for my hubris. Three minutes later, while I was still feeling quite pleased with myself for being such a sly puss about those drawings, Jane walked in, her face immobile. "Ev," she said, "guess what?"

"What? I give up."

"There are these here pictures of our bungalow in San Sebo. I'm dying to get them. I must be dying to get them, because Ned Hertwood told me I was."

I was trying to think of something to say, but Jane said it for me. "You nit," she explained, her face still frozen, "you won't give up, will you? You're up to something again, aren't you? What is it this time?"

"I'm not sure. I'll find out after I get the pictures."

"That's what I'm afraid of, that you'll find out. Wouldn't you rather maybe not find out? Just for a change?"

As a matter of fact, Jane was absolutely right: I would rather not find out. But if I had been somebody's patsy, if some innocent people had been at one extreme killed and at the other made fools of, I wanted to know. Even though I hated the idea of what I might find out. "Yes," I said. "Yes, dear, but there's nothing I can do about it. I've got to know."

SEVENTEEN

While I waited for the drawings to arrive, assuming that they would arrive, I had no choice but to go to work, which, as any honest people who work in advertising—if you can find them—will assure you is a terrible thing. I bellowed. "Saaallly! Come on in for a second, will you?"

Sally came in, crisp and gimlet-eyed. "No need to shout, Ev. I'm overworked, incompetent, and probably senile, but not deaf. Unfortunately."

"Oh, come on, what'd I do now?"

"Nothing much. And that's the trouble. You've been moping about so much these last weeks that you haven't got a blessed thing worth mentioning done. I don't really care, but it's up to me to hold off the world and make excuses for you. When you finally get to it, if you do, you'll start lashing me to go faster and faster like I was Man O' War or somebody."

I corrected her: "Woman O' War. Okay, I'll try to keep it to a gentle trot. What's the worst we've got waiting?"

"Never mind the 'we.' And everything's the worst. You name it, you got it."

"All right. If you're going to be like that just tell me what's the first of the worst?"

"This morning's appointment. At eleven. The perfume people."

"Okay. I've still got some time. I'll go over the research and we'll be ready for them."

"*You'll* be ready for them." She put the research folder on my desk and went out. "I'll stop all phone calls and close your door. Now you go to work."

I opened the folder. It was an omen. I had been scooting around like a toy balloon losing air, juggling four candidates for murderer before, as Jane was only too eager to tell me, I had a murder for them to have committed. The perfume job was very much like that, only in the wonderful world of advertising it made sense. We had a study going to figure out how women felt about buying our client's product, which sounds reasonable, except that this was before the client had a product for them to buy (should any of them be so foolish as to want to buy it once it was given birth to).

Such is standard procedure in advertising, though, and in its own perverted way it makes good sense. The product was perfume, and even though it may sound strange, perfume is least of all a scent. Mainly it's a liquid that imparts a new dimension to the flesh it lands on—sexiness, virginity, dominance, mystery, sin—whatever the wearer wants. And what the wearer wants changes with the times. My job was to find out what the ladies of the 1980's wanted out of their perfumes and tell the client about it.

Then the client's job was to go to his chemistry lab and whip up a batch of something that would do the trick. To be more specific, if this were the eighteenth century, when the kids needed something to divert attention from the fact that they none of them hopped in the tub very often, not even on Saturday night, the client would probably develop something that smelled like laundry bleach. Maybe a powerful number like Meltdown or Blastoff would have won a big order from Louis the Fourteenth. Or again, in a more modest era, items like Flower Garden or American Beauty Rose or Meadowlark might have made a young maid feel that her perfume was transforming her into something fresh and wholesome and innocent.

"Mrs. Partridge and Mr. Tiani are here," Sally announced at eleven on the nose.

"Hi, come in. How are you, Leona, Harry? Grab a couple of chairs." Leona Partridge and Harry Tiani were respectively marketing director and chief chemist for LaVerne Fragrances. (As the name might have cued you in, the company did not cater to the most exclusive of markets.) "What say we go over this stuff and then I've booked us a table, if you're free for lunch."

"Sure, love it."

"Fine with me."

"Good. Let's get our coffee set, and then I'll show you what we've got. Sorry we don't have a full presentation worked up as yet."

"Forget it," Leona said. "We know we're rushing you, but we're anxious to get into production."

They were anxious to get into production and they hadn't even developed the scent. It was going to take them six months to produce it, plus a couple more for consumer tests, deciding on the packaging—which usually costs more than the perfume itself—and getting the advertising and marketing plans together. But clients have to beat up on somebody, and that's what their advertising agencies are for. They the beaters and we the beatees; they get rid of their bile and we get rid of their billions. It's nature's way of keeping the world in balance.

"Okay, let's look." We gathered around some sheets I had scribbled on with a red pencil. "Items in the sex area don't compute these days, unless all you want is the puberty market. It looks like sex is just an ordinary something you tear off absentmindedly while you're waiting for the bus. Sex is ho-hum, God help us. So you can scratch anything that smells like Seduction, Love Nest, and Beddybye from the list."

"I knew it," the Partridge said.

She didn't, but clients need to let you understand that you can't possibly tell them anything at all about their business. Tiani, the chemist, kept his mouth shut; one-upmanship with ad agencies isn't required for a technician's mental health.

"Now that sin is old hat, at least sexwise," I went on, "it looks like the kinky is in. Crime, drugs, and like that. You know, like Opium and Poison."

Partridge nodded. "Obsession."

"Right. Obsession is sexy, but it's kinky sexy. Kinky sexy is good."

"You got that, Harry?" Leona asked Tiani.

He looked bored. "So I'll take the old Carnation, maybe throw in a little musk, some more spice. I don't know. What the hell. Yeah, I got it."

"Not so fast, Harry," I said. "This kinky business divides into two different market segments. First, there are the ladies who are saying to the fellows that they've arrived, they've made it, and they can be as weird as the next guy. They want the product to smell like Far Out, or Dig This. You know what I'm saying?"

They both nodded, and I went on. "Then there's the more extreme women who want something that says more than just that they've made it. They want to give it out that they're about to take over and beat up on the boys. You know: leather, whips, spiky orange hair. For them, in crescendoing order, the product has to be like My Turn, Submit, or Take That! That sort of stuff. When we get down to picking names, we should be thinking about handles like Blackmail or Heist. Even Eat It, with two exclamation points."

"Eat It?" Tiani asked, looking surprised. "So what do I do, add pickle juice?"

"That'd be the least of it, honey," Leona the P leered.

We went to lunch anyway.

Maybe this makes it clear what I mean: If I could draw a salary for measuring the likelihood that consumers will buy something before it even exists, then why couldn't I decide that somebody was a murderer before I knew that a murder had been committed? (I'm not at all sure I'd want anybody to answer that question.)

EIGHTEEN

After that, there was only work to keep me occupied while I waited to hear from Ned Hertwood. I hunkered down, nose to the computer, coming up for air and martinis only as absolutely necessary for my health. Finally, one morning's mail brought a large brown envelope with stamps bearing the images of Sarge and Elizabeth II looking at each other as equals, and with equal distaste. On second thought, the lady's distaste was the winner; it takes centuries of breeding to project genteel disapproval with such elegance, and Sarge wasn't up to the mark.

There was a scribbled note from Ned Hertwood. "Here they are. The boy says this is what you were after, and this is all of it. And thanks for putting me on to the lad. He's terrific. We've bought some of his new ones ourselves. Regards from us both, and come see us in London. Best to Jane."

There was a postscript: "Your friend Doc is still missing, but Juleen is getting along somehow. Not to worry." I checked the contents, counted half a dozen sketches of bungalows, including the one with the rotted mango, beaches, and palm trees. I re-enveloped them, deciding that in the relative peace and quiet of home that evening I could try to puzzle out what I thought they could tell me about life and death in San Sebo. Was it just a child's game, like the funny paper pictures I used to grab that told me to look for sixteen hidden pussycats in the sketch of a grove of trees? Probably. Jane would have thought so, and Jane is usually right.

That evening Jane, Billy, and I gathered around, the three of us on the couch, the pictures spread out on the coffee table. "Okay," Billy said, "so it's a bunch of huts and palm trees. Now what, Sherlock?"

"I'm waiting for your fresh insights, kid. They taught me in school that little children always bring fresh insights into the grown-up world." Almost the only way I could do battle with fourteen-year-old Billy was to let him know I pegged him in the little children category, which killed the boy.

"Yeah?"

"Yeah."

"And they had gas light and candles in the auditorium when you was in school, Pops. And girls in gym bloomers."

"'When you *were* in school,'" Jane interjected. "And there's nothing wrong with gym bloomers. Your grandmother wore them and the pictures of her are lovely."

"I'll bet," the boy said. "How'd Ev look in 'em?"

"Better'n you," I said feebly.

The kid looked thoughtful. "I'll go along with that."

"Hah, hah." I didn't stick my tongue out, though.

Jane slammed a hand down on the coffee table. "Stop it, you two. Are we going to look at the pictures or not?"

"Ah, ma, we don't even know what we're looking for. Ev's just got a burr up his—"

"Stop it!"

"—flea in his ear."

I can be a child too, if I'm pressed, and sometimes it

doesn't take much pressing. "All right," I said, "let's skip it. I'll look at them myself after dinner." I gathered them up in a furious sweep, and two slithered off the table onto the floor. Billy snickered.

One picture landed wrong side up, and I glanced at the back as I retrieved it. It was a scrap from the hospital, one of the precious pieces of paper the boy and Doc were able to get hold of for drawing on. "San Sebo General Hospital," was the heading.

"Wait a sec," I said. "Let's kiss and make up and take a peek at the backs. Maybe that'll tell us something."

It was Jane who found it. "Look at this," she urged. "I think it's an autopsy report that they threw out. And it's for a white male, elderly. How many autopsies on white males, elderly, do you think they do down there? I can't read the name, it's been blotted out, but what do you think? It's just got to be Henry Olds, doesn't it?"

I grabbed the paper. "Lemme see. I'd say so. They're sure clearing room in the files mighty quick if it is, though." I squinted my way down the page. "Hey, look. They found a fortune in alcohol tucked away on the inside, if I'm reading this right. That's gotta be Henry Olds."

Jane looked where I was pointing. "Uh huh. And pentobarbitol sodium. Sounds like a tranquilizer."

We looked at each other. "Henry wasn't the type for tranquilizers," I said, while simultaneously Jane said, "If it is, alcohol and tranquilizers together could kill somebody a lot younger than old Henry."

"You know," Jane said, "this is what the police were looking for in Doc's cottage, I'll bet. That's why they tore the pictures off the wall and took all little Andy's drawings."

"I think so too," I said. "And I think Sarge told the hospital to get rid of this report. No murders for Sarge; bad for business. But instead of destroying it they gave it to the kid for his drawings, just like always."

"And Sarge found out. And sent the police to get it back."

We sat quietly, brooding over the significance of our find. I broke the silence. "Okay, my dear," I said, "you said I was going around finding murderers when I didn't have a murder. How about it now? What've I don't got now?"

"Dinner, for one thing," Billy said. "That's what I don't got. And I'm hungry."

We both ignored the boy, and for Jane to give preference to me when her precious is bellowing for his slops constitutes a milestone. "I don't know," she said slowly. "Maybe you're right. Maybe you've got a murder at last. I don't know. But I'm not so sure you've found a murderer. That's what you've don't got now."

"I'll work on it, I'll work on it," I said defensively.

"Don't you dare," Jane warned me, but I wasn't listening. "Tell me something," I asked.

"I'll tell you something," Billy put in. "There's rice burning. I can smell it. And I'm not gonna scrape it off the bottom of the pan, either," he yelled after my retreating back as I scooted into the kitchen on the double. "It's not my fault!"

I chucked the rice and put on water for spaghetti; you can always shut a kid up with spaghetti. In fact, you can generally shut me up with spaghetti. I walked back into the living room with infinite dignity. "Dinner will be fifteen minutes late, if that's all right with Your Highness."

"Why should I mind?" the kid groused. "I'll probably be dead by then."

"Both of you cut it out," Jane warned. "I'm tired of this."

"Ah, heck, ma," Billy said, "you know Ev and me like to kid around. Doesn't mean a thing."

"Ev and *I*," Jane corrected mechanically.

"Come on, Jane," I put in. "It doesn't mean anything, and you know it."

"Okay, okay. Let's drop it. Let's go back to the beginning. You said I should tell you something. What should I tell you?"

"Yeah. What I mean is, if somebody put old Henry to sleep, do you think it's maybe a little more likely to decide that somebody extended the same courtesy to Mrs. Henry?"

Jane pursed her lips. "I'll buy that."

"And that it's the same somebody in both cases?"

She added a frown to the pursed lips, putting her whole lovely face into the act. "Probably. Or almost probably."

"I'd make it probably probably, not almost."

"You're probably right."

"It's probably fifteen minutes now," Billy said, "if anybody wants to know."

"Holy cow!" I ran into the kitchen. I came back into the living room and tried, with some small success, to look cool and unconcerned. "You two feel like eating Chinese tonight? I feel like it. What say we go up to 86th and find a good Chinese restaurant?"

"86th is German," Billy grumbled.

"We'll find Chinese," I promised.

We went out. We went to 86th. We found Chinese. Sometimes I win. Or else sometimes the boy lets me win, to give me false hopes.

NINETEEN

On the way back from the restaurant, my stomach comfortably loaded, I thought over all the tiny pieces I had been collecting. Ned Hertwood and his stay in the hospital, or, as he put it, in hospital. The autopsy report on the back of little Andy's sketch of the bungalow. The likelihood that I knew now that there was indeed a murder or two to think about. The fact that I still had a minimum of four candidates for murderer left to choose among.

I thought about it all the next day. Then, after work, as Jane and I were turning the key to get into the apartment, I said, "Hey, listen, I've got a couple of ideas about this San Sebo business that I want to lay on you and Billy tonight, see what you make of them."

"Ah, look, Ev," Jane said, "Billy'll make hash of them,

that's what. Why don't you leave the boy out? I hate to see the two of you bicker."

"It doesn't mean anything, dear. We both like it. Besides, this time it won't happen. I've got things worked out too well for Billy to be able to get at me."

Dinner completed, and without burned rice, dissolved spaghetti, or anything else disastrous, I began. "Billy boy," I said, "I need your help."

"Right, old timer. Shoot."

I opened my yawp to resent that, but snapped it shut instead. "Okay. If I got so sick that I needed to be taken off in an ambulance, and you had to tell somebody where I was, what would you say?"

"I'd say like they took Ev to Mount Sinai."

"Yeah. Let's say you didn't know where exactly I was. Then what'd you say."

"'Ev's in some hospital, but I don't know which one.' How's that?"

"Good. Fine. But not what I'm after. I'll begin the sentence, and you finish it. You'd say, 'Ev's in—' Go ahead, say it, son."

Billy looked at me with something between scorn and confusion. "All right, you asked for it. I'll say it. 'Ev's in the nuthouse. He's in the funny farm. They put this jacket on him and took him off. Lawsamercy but you shoulda heard the racket!'"

"Jane!" I bellowed, "he's starting up with me!"

"This time it won't happen, huh?" Jane asked. "Now hear this, you two. You will knock it off right now. Not another word from either of you." She turned to me. "I'll handle this myself. What do you want?"

"Just ask the boy a simple question for me. "If somebody was sick and you didn't know what hospital they were in, what would you say if you were asked where he was?"

"Billy," Jane commanded, "can you answer that?"

With great, great weariness, Billy said, "Ooh, that's so hard!" He caught the look on his mother's face, and hurried

1 1 7

on to say, "I'd say he's in the hospital but I don't know which one."

"Thank you. Thank you very much for your cooperation, Billy." I was all dignity. "And Ned Hertwood and anybody else from England would say 'He's in hospital,' not 'in *the* hospital.' That's the way they put it over there. Right?"

"Right," Jane said. "If you say so."

"Whaddya mean, 'if I say so.' Am I right or am I wrong?"

"Tell him he's right, ma. It's easier that way."

"All right. That's it. You two win." I withdrew and picked up the television listing, all dignity. If I had been Sarge I would have called in the General Assembly.

"Come on, Ev," Jane said. "Don't get sore. Just unwind and let's go on."

I waited a full ten seconds to see if she planned on adding anything about both her children, but she didn't, so I allowed myself to be mollified. "Thank you," I said. "Thank you both ever so much." I cleared my throat. "All right, then, now let's consider the note that Dolly Lamoureux says she got while she was out picnicking with Lizzie Olds. What'd it say?" I held up a hand. "Never mind, I'll tell you. It said that her husband was in hospital, not in *the* hospital. Ergo, and Q.E.D., the note was written by somebody from England."

"Oh, I don't know," Jane said. "It could just be a tele-graphic way of writing an emergency note when you're in a hurry."

"Yeah," Billy added, "like, Help. Ev Franklin off rocker."

"I'll overlook that," I said, "and won't even consider giving you a good bust in chops. Can we go on?" I turned back to Jane. "Maybe. But the rest of the note wasn't telegraphese. It read, 'Your husband is very ill,' not 'Your husband ill.' It's not consistent."

Jane looked doubtful. "I'm not convinced, but for the sake of argument, I'll buy it for now. What comes next, as if I didn't know."

"You know, all right, don't you?"

"You mean Loretta Holland, because she's from England. So now what? You can't make a federal case out of somebody's grammar, especially when you don't even have the note, just your recollection of Dolly Lamoureux's recollection of how it read. Assuming Dolly got it right, or even that she was telling the truth to begin with."

"Good points. Well taken, but go along with me anyway, just for now."

"Do I have a choice?" She paused, looking weary. "Go ahead, then."

"I'll tell you what, Jane. I won't do a thing. Not really, except maybe buzz Ned Hertwood on San Sebo—I hope he took a couple of weeks there—and ask him to find out one thing for me. What I'd like him to do is ask little Andy a question, that's all."

"What question?"

"You remember the kid wanted to do a sketch of the big lady who was fighting? What I want to know is if the big lady who was fighting hit anybody with a stick, and if the answer's yes, I'd like to get a description of that stick. I mean, all large American women may look more or less alike to the kid, but I'll bet he can tell one stick from another. The boy's got an artist's eye, no?"

"What kind of a stick?"

"What I'm hoping—and I won't give Ned any hints—is that Andy saw one economy size woman smack another of the same with a slim, round stick, white or off-white, and maybe he'll tell us it was smooth and shiny and about so long." I enclosed a space of about ten inches between my open hands.

"Sounds like an outsize toothpick. Or a baton for a midget cheer leader. What are you aiming at?"

"I'm aiming at something right here in this house, right in my suitcase, where I left it after we unpacked. A white plastic knitting needle. I can practically see somebody arguing with Elizabeth Olds, and the Olds woman refusing to pay attention and pretending to be concerned with nothing except her knitting. I can see someone getting damned mad at that, someone who isn't used to being ignored, like maybe Loretta Holland, grabbing the knitting out of the old girl's hands and jabbing her in the arm with the needle. Someone in a rage acting on impulse."

"You sure can see a lot, honey bunch."

"You know what else I can see?" From the look on Jane's face I concluded it would be best to plunge ahead without waiting for a reply. "I can see that needle in the suitcase, still just as dirty as it was when I packed it. And you know what? There's something else that dingy brown color besides plain dirt."

"What?"

"Plain blood."

"At last something we can check."

We did. It was.

I figured I was finally on to something.

But then it's always brightest just before the dark, right?

TWENTY

I reached Ned by phone while he was still lazing on the shores of the island paradise, but it didn't add much, if anything, to what I already knew. He was back to me in half a day to report that little Andy was vague on the subject of the knitting needle, and that unless Ned had been prepared to feed the boy his lines, there wasn't much he could have gotten out of him. And the big lady who fought was nothing more than a big lady who fought, neither young nor old nor fat nor thin. Just white, which apparently was sufficiently ridiculous in itself to wipe out all other identifying characteristics.

But at least, for what it was worth, I knew that there was blood on the knitting needle. What the empty sugar bags I had also inherited from Doc might signify, I still had no idea. I lay them aside in the musty attic of my mind.

Nor was it clear what, if anything, I ought to be doing next, so I went to work at the job Finch, etc., was paying me to do. Sometimes I think work is what I do when I can't think of a more profitable way to occupy my mind. It occurred to me that the Pebble Beach meetings would be coming up in another six weeks, and that if I thought of a way to confront, or at least confound, Madam Holland, I could put it into effect at that time. For the moment though the only plan that suggested itself was to look the lady in the eye and demand, "Why did you slay Mr. and Mrs. Henry Olds, you servant of Satan?" I had heard as a child that criminals, basically cowards, could be expected to avert their eyes and cringe in a corner when faced with a forthright challenge. (I had also been informed that a manly and unflinching gaze would similarly conquer mad dogs and ravening beasts, though that might appear less relevant to the current situation.)

Unfortunately, work proved so painful that I shifted back to sleuthing. I had been requested by top management to develop a position paper assessing the potential for a new mode of advertising that some warped genius had announced to a jaded communications industry. What every advertiser prays for is a medium for his message that will trap the audience and hold a hapless consumer's attention long enough for the purchase proposition to sink in, and to a list which already included elevators and the interiors of taxicabs, someone had just added the stalls in public restrooms, giving an added and poignant significance to the concept of invasion of privacy.

I uncovered my typewriter and banged out "Potential for Restroom Advertising." After ten minutes of gnawing at a hangnail, I XXX'd out the heading and tapped sufficient keys to create, "Get in touch with Sarge?" Then I walked down to Jane's office, called out, "See ya later," and went to a movie. It was in Portuguese, and very much en vogue among fashionable cineasts. I don't understand Portuguese, but then there was very little I was understanding at the moment, so I enjoyed it very much, I think.

The next morning I looked at the message in the typewriter and decided it was too terrible to contemplate. Getting in touch with Sarge was as attractive an idea as hailing the prospect of advertising in public johns. Either one might lead to further intrusions on a body's privacy: Sarge might return the contact, and my landlord might put a TV monitor in the bathroom at home to display periodic messages like, "Good guys pay their rent on the first."

As it happened, an article in the morning *Times* gave me another idea, and it concerned my all-time favorite debutante. When I was a kid I would come across headlines on the society page that read something like, "Charity Balls This Season's Big Success," or "Society Enthuses over Charity Balls." I thought—and be generous; I wasn't even a teenager yet—that there was some dumb old debutante named Charity Balls, which didn't seem too illogical. Charity Balls: I could visualize a demure young lady, sweet, with wispy blonde hair, speaking in a softly musical voice. I even wondered if she'd be my date when I grew up. Oh, my sweet Charity, how I adored you!

Here it was again. This time it read, "Media Magnate and Wife Sponsor Charity Ball." Randolph and Loretta. I suppose it meant that Holland was planning something vicious in the world of high finance and that his Public Relations consultants had told him to help a charity, any charity, unmarried puppy dogs, arthritic goldfish, anything, and they'd make sure he got appropriate press coverage even in papers and on TV stations he didn't own. More to the point, it meant that the Hollands were in New York, sweeping the floor of the Waldorf ballroom and sticking paper roses on the walls with transparent tape, getting ready for their blast, laughing and shoving each other as they did so, all awash with their own goodness.

I got their address, which isn't as easy as it sounds, from Ed Jorgensen's secretary. There was no way for me to call and invite myself over, so I decided to run into Loretta Holland accidentally on the street, and get myself invited up. The paper said that Madam was staying in town to supervise the preparations for Miss Balls—Oops!—while Mister was at their Connecticut place. I figured she'd be unable to drag herself out of the apartment before 10 A.M., so I practiced walking past the Hollands's building beginning at 10 on Saturday.

And on Sunday. And then on Saturday again. Jane was considering divorce, but I bribed her with a promise to do all the grocery shopping for the household on my way home each day, which was to be between 12:30 and 1 P.M.

I lucked out on the second Sunday. "Why, Mrs. Holland!" I gasped in insincere astonishment. "What a surprise!"

It took her a moment to recognize me, or at least she pretended it took her a moment. "Mr. Franklin. How nice," she lied.

"I'm terribly glad to see you," I trilled, "because there was something I needed to talk to you about, and I was planning to contact you anyway. Do you have five, ten, minutes to talk?" She hesitated, so I added, "It's about Sarge. I've got a message he insisted I deliver to you personally. You remember Sarge. San Sebo?"

The dawn of a false recognition lit her face. "Oh, yes, of course." She looked at her watch, a slight squint indicating that among Loretta Holland's other naughty little secrets was a pair of unused reading glasses. I thought it possible that that could be the secret that troubled her the most. "I *do* have an appointment, but perhaps a few minutes— Why don't you come up?"

I assented, and marched like a little soldier into the dragon lady's lair.

The elevator opened directly into the foyer of the Hollands's duplex; they occupied the only apartment on the floor. Mrs. H swept into the living room while I tumbled about awkwardly in her wake, figurative hat in hand. The room was large, panelled, and decorated in an Englishy way that I was certain had enabled at least one happy interior decorator to move permanently to Capri and raise flowers or small boys, as his fancy took him. No, the oils that graced the walls were not Cézannes or Monets. Somebody, and I suspect Loretta herself, had decided that if only second string works by first place artists could be obtained, they would quite simply be too déclassé, no matter how fine in appearance. Instead the lady had opted for the very finest of American regional paintings, and the Hudson River School—Inness, Church, Kensett—presided over the premises. After all, they cost enough in their own rights, and, my dear, the ostentation of a Renoir or a Seurat would have been too vulgar, don't you think?

"We'll have some tea, Henrietta," she said to a maid. "In here." She didn't ask me if I wanted tea, but then I shouldn't criticize; after all, the lady had only a single blind spot that I knew of, even if it did encompass most of the several billions of people on Planet Earth.

She sat back, nestling into a scatter of cushions, and waved me vaguely into a brocaded wing chair. "Now then, Mr. Franklin, you said something about a message from—Sarge, is it? Did I get that right?"

"That's right." As you know damn well, I thought.

"How strange. He was that pompous little man who arrested poor Dolly Lamoureux, wasn't he? I remember now." Her laughter tinkled lightly, the most delicate of Baccarat crystal pinged by a lacquered fingernail. "What on earth could he have to tell me? Did Randy skip out on our hotel bill?" The Baccarat rang daintily again.

Tea arrived, and I thereby received a moment's grace to figure out what I could possibly answer. I had blurted out that line about Sarge simply to hold the woman once I had finally managed to make contact. I took a deep breath and plunged in; maybe this barracuda would be kinder to me than another one was to Elizabeth Olds. "I was down on San Sebo for a weekend. One of those four day, three night packages. You know?"

She looked dryly at me. "Oh? How nice. And Mr. Sarge asked you to say aloha to me? Is that it?" She smiled, not, fortunately, showing any teeth as she did so.

Well, what the hell, if I was going to make an ass of myself, I might as well skip over the equine variety and go right for the economy, or elephantine, package. "Not exactly. He, uh, asked me to suggest to you that the last payment you sent was a tad late in arriving. He'd appreciate it if you could try being more nearly on time. That's all."

She looked blank, but the cords alongside her cheeks stood out for a moment. I may not have hit a bullseye, but something encouraged Loretta Holland to clench her teeth, however briefly. "Mr. Franklin," she said softly, "I don't have the slightest idea what you're talking about. Please don't play games. I have neither the time nor the inclination."

"I think you know what I mean, Mrs. Holland. It's about the note that Dolly Lamoureux got. The one you sent, saying her husband was in the hospital. Sarge got hold of it, as we both know, and he's blackmailing you." Talk about going out on limbs!

"The note *I* sent? Are you so sure? I thought that nobody knew if there was such a note, much less who wrote it. I think it might be wise if you left now, Mr. Franklin, before either one of us says something we might both regret. Though," she added, "you've reached that point already, haven't you?"

"Not necessarily, Mrs. Holland. Sarge has admitted, quite cheerfully, that he has the note and that you're paying him to keep quiet about it. No need to be upset; all I'm saying is that you don't have to buy silence from the man. He'll do anything to avoid upsetting the tourist trade with tales of mayhem and murder, and that even includes giving up a little blackmail on the side. After all, I doubt very much the loss of whatever you're sending comes anywhere near what it would be if something cut into the man's sacred tourist dollars." Talk about flying blind! I was amazed that I could say all that without stammering.

Those lovely jaw muscles clenched again. "I understand now. The key word is 'blackmail,' isn't it. You think you know something that's worth money to me, don't you. I'm amazed and ashamed, and I'll ask you to leave my apartment. If you're lucky I shan't say anything to my husband. Whatever made you think you could do it, get away with such nonsense! A man in your position!"

"I'm glad you asked me that. First, let me assure you I want nothing from you. No blackmail. No money. Is that clear?" She nodded coldly, unconvinced, her lips pressed together, an inquisitor sitting in judgment. "Second, I've seen the note," I added, stretching the truth a shade, "and the wording is one only an Englishman—or Englishwoman—

would use." I went into my routine on 'in hospital' vs. 'in the hospital.' "And then there's the handwriting; it's yours, Mrs. Holland. I've seen a note you sent to Ed Jorgensen down at the meetings, and the writing is the same."

She smiled. She sat back against the cushions and relaxed. I knew I had made a mistake. Somehow I had wandered off course; the Geiger counter of guilt was beginning to beep more faintly. I wondered if the note had been printed in block letters or even typed. Whatever it was I had lost the edge. "Really. That's interesting. Tell me, had it ever occurred to you that I wasn't the only one in our party brought up in England? I defer to your superior knowledge of graphology and what it indicates about the handwriting on this note of yours"—here she bowed graciously—"and I admit I'm delighted by your building a criminal case out of the absence of the definite article, but I suggest, for your own good, that you look elsewhere for your villain." She pursed her lips, amused as all hell. "Perhaps inside yourself?"

"But you were the only one of us born in England, the only one who'd say 'in hospital.'" Was I on the run? Getting defensive?

"Was I, Mr. Franklin?"

"Weren't you?"

"As the children in both England and America would put it, I asked you first. Think hard."

"Well, there's only—you can't possibly be suggesting Kenny! Not Ken Tillson!" She smiled in silence and waited for me to wiggle a shade more on the hook. "You'd try to throw guilt on your own friend, simply to take care of yourself?"

"I try to throw guilt on nobody. I don't think there's any guilt to throw, and I don't think you do either. What do you take me for!"

I thought about Loretta Holland. What did I take her for, this self-involved, self-adoring woman, this shining center of her privately constructed universe. "I take you," I said slowly, "for a woman who may mean no particular harm, who may not be petty or vindictive, but who nevertheless sees as the major problem of the day, the issue transcending other questions of good, evil, war, or peace, whether or not her hams have expanded a quarter of an inch or drooped an eighth of an inch and to what extent this will affect her squeezing them attractively into a Valentino gown when she hosts her charity bash at the Waldorf next week."

"Nicely put. Except it's at the Plaza." She leaned forward. "Very well, my lad. You've been frank. As I used to say in the days when I thought Valentino was a dead movie star, you've put your ass on the table, and the least I can do is to do likewise. Now you listen to me."

She opened a silver cigarette box, one with a malachite lid, and lit up. She jetted out a stream of smoke that cut a hole in the air like steam escaping under pressure. A strand of hair fell across her face, possibly the first such dereliction from perfection that had beset Loretta Holland's person since she had become Randolph's wife. Brushing the errant lock aside irritably, she stood and strode over to the fireplace to lean against the mantel. Something of the animal fire that had made her a top model a dozen years ago boiled to the surface as she posed there, looking at me hard.

"Now you listen," she repeated. "You're right about one thing: I don't want trouble. I can't afford it in my position. But you're wrong if you think I won't or can't fight it. I don't know what you're after, but let me tell you I'm not going to make it easy for you. I may look like a china doll to you, chum, but don't underestimate me. Don't start anything you're not able to finish."

I forebore mentioning that in no way did she look like a china doll to me. Steel doll was more like it. Steel doll chilled in the freezer overnight.

"Whatever I've got I've gotten the hard way," she said. Her mouth twisted into the mockery of a smile. "Or as I understand they put it in England, I've *got* the hard way. Listen to me. I used to be Loretta Saunders. There must have been a thousand generations of Saunders living in a little village in Norfolk. Thorpe Abbotts. Nobody ever left it or even got further than the nearest market town. That was Diss, if you'd like all the details."

I nodded, not because I wanted a geography lesson, but because I wanted the story to go on. It did. "My granddad—that was Albert Saunders—took in laundry from the American airbase nearby, the 100th Bomb Group, to be precise. Eighth Air Force. And that's what the Saunders must have done forever, take in laundry. Knut Saunders did the wash for the Norsemen, Lucius Gaius Saunders for the Romans, and Pierre Saunders for the Normans. They were always in demand, the Saunders. Needed. To do laundry. In Thorpe Abbotts." She laughed.

"I don't see—" I began.

"Shut up," she snapped. "No one interrupts Mrs. Randolph Holland. Didn't you know that? And I don't give a damn what you do or don't see." She jammed out her butt on a bronze hunting dog snarling forever on the mantel, and turned back to me. "It took a world war to get my parents out of Thorpe Abbotts and away from the smell of bleach and laundry soap. They liked it in London, German bombs or no. And so did I when I was old enough to appreciate the difference. It was too late for them, but little Loretta was supposed to go far. They had plans. I started training as a nurse, a favorite way for a youngster with little education and no family connections to get a leg up in the world that England used to be."

"You poor thing," I murmured sympathetically. "All those awful sick people. Do you have to tell me about it, though? Should I feel sorry? Should I admire what you've made of yourself? Because I'm afraid I don't, Mrs. Holland."

"I'm devastated," she returned, "but bear with me a moment more. You really know the rest, anyway. Someone saw me—the details don't matter—I never finished my training as a nurse, and I became a model. A damned good one, too. Then I married Randy. So don't feel sorry, and for God's sake don't admire me either. The thought is sickening. Just be a little bit afraid of me, Mr. Franklin. I've worked and fought for what I've got and no one is going to spoil it for me with cheap tricks and shabby stabs at blackmail. I'm surprised your mommy didn't teach you to stick to your *own* knitting. You could get stuck with the needle playing with someone else's yarn, you know." She smiled, but nastily. "Do you understand that?"

She didn't say she'd kill, but that was the impression I figured she wanted both of us to get. "Perfectly," I answered. "Poor Elizabeth Olds, so old, so ugly, and so full of cheap tricks that could get in a lady's way. And possibly poor me, threatening scandal and odd items like simple justice. And not to overlook anybody, there's nasty, vindictive Henry Olds, so full of his own cheap tricks, not to mention so full of pentobarbitol sodium. Isn't that right?"

For the first time she looked flustered. "Pentobar—?" Her expression segued from confusion to amazement to delight, and she finished by breaking into laughter raucous enough to crack her makeup, if it hadn't cost her fifty bucks an ounce. She couldn't talk for laughing, and she couldn't stay on her feet, but threw herself into a chair, slumped down on her spine, her legs akimbo in a mode more befitting one of the thousand years of Saunders girls than Mrs. Randolph Holland.

The maid came charging in to investigate the fireworks. Loretta still could only gasp a few words, but managed to communicate by flipping her wrist toward the door and indicating between the gales of merriment that I was to be shown out. I waited in the foyer for the elevator and wondered what had brought on the hysteria.

As the elevator brought me down and deposited my plebian frame beneath the watchful eye of the doorman, I concluded that Loretta Holland hadn't been the least bit hysterical. She had found something genuinely funny, something that rated an attack of merriment so fierce as to border on the brutal, something that had to do with the deaths of Henry and Elizabeth Olds. I'll say one thing: This must have been the first time in fifty years that either of the Olds kids had brought happiness into the life of another, especially when that other was rich, beautiful, and the wife of a business associate. But how or why was something else, something I was unable even to speculate about, at least not for the moment. I sighed; nothing was getting clearer, only muddier.

TWENTY-ONE

I had drawn a blank with Loretta Holland. I had both infuri-
ated her and reduced her to helpless laughter for reasons I
had no way of fathoming. She had also done her best to hint
that somebody else, probably Ken Tillson, had sent that note
to Dolly Lamoureux while she was picnicking with Lizzie
Olds. If there was a note.

I needed two things. A rest, and more information about
that note. If there was a note. If there was a note.

It looked to me as if I could take care of both needs by a
fast trip to San Sebo. The newspapers did indeed have ads for
glamorous weekends, four days and three nights under a
tropic moon, at bargain rates. (Free rum cocktail at airport on
arrival, manager's party with delicious hors d'oeuvres, native
dancing to delight the eye, duty free shops, etc., etc.)

Fortunately, I had some compensatory time coming to me

for having worked a number of weekends, so there was no need to use up any vacation time to get the third day of that tempting package. Compensatory time is a marvelous institution, though only from the boss's point of view. The idea is that lower paid workers get money for putting in overtime, the lucky stiffs, but so-called executives get compensatory time, time off to make up for the extra hours. Only they're not supposed to take it; they're supposed to be suffused with a warm glow of satisfaction at having done their jobs; professional pride is presumed to be enough reward, and never mind such piddling considerations as compensatory time.

I had my own philosophy about this point of view: Screw professional pride. I want my time off. When I first came to New York I got a job at a department store, in their marketing division. I'm so ashamed for them that I'll leave out their name and say only that it rhymes with Lacy's. They told me I was an executive, and bursting with pride I communicated the exhilarating news to my parents upstate. I soon found out that what made my kind of executive an executive was four things: I got paid less than union workers; I was privileged to ride the less crowded executive elevator up to the office floors, an elevator that went up on alternate Thursdays unless it was out of order, which it frequently was; I got compensatory time for working late instead of real money; and I was expected to forego, as a professional, laying claim to my compensatory time.

As I say, Screw that.

I told Jane I was going down to San Sebo for the weekend but only in the interests of seeing that justice was done.

"Oh, no," Jane said. "Never mind this justice business. If you're going to San Sebo, so'm I. For one thing, somebody's got to keep you out of trouble, and for another, I tan better than you do."

Naturally, Billy was listening. "So do I. When do we leave?"

I sighed. "You two think we're made of money?"

They answered affirmatively. My sole glimmer of victory was winning the decision to get only one room with twin beds and a cot. (Third member of same family only $10 more a day in one room, the ad cooed seductively.) Of course I lived to regret my triumph because Billy turned in so much later than I did that I never got enough sleep. What's more, his hair lotions, brushes, and assorted teenage cosmetics, the necromantic purposes of which I scarce dared contemplate, left no room for spreading out my own laughable collection on either dresser tops or bathroom sink. Sometimes I think my wife and her son are experts in guerrilla warfare.

Before we left I made a copy of that autopsy report on the elderly white male whose innards were laced with such generous helpings of pentobarbitol sodium.

The hotel was not in the luxury class of the one that had housed the board meetings, but aside from the noise wafting in from windows facing the island's electric generating plant, it was adequate. Billy, the snob, sneered a bit at the accommodations. I explained to him that an even, constant, whirring sound was considered by many to be soothing, that it was called "white noise," and that it was very much favored by insomniacs for its sleep-inducing qualities.

The boy thought about it, and then announced, "Yeah? Well, I know another sound like that. It's called 'cheep, cheep.'"

"Don't you get fresh with Ev, you hear?" Jane commanded.

"Aw, ma, I was just tellin' it like it is, man."

"As it is. And don't call me man, boy."

I smirked, carefully hiding my leer of triumph from Jane. Nevertheless I was so annoyed that my sleep was cut into even more at night as I lay awake listening to that presumably deliciously relaxing white noise wafting through the window of our room, damn it.

Our first morning I sashayed impudently over to Government House and asked for Sarge. He looked at me equivocally as I was ushered into his office. I looked not at him directly, but at that old familiar T-shirt, delicately unwashed and antiqued as it was by food, sweat, and tears. Possibly it was still in deep mourning for the recently deceased guests who had almost certainly passed on before spending all their tourist dollars. "Well," he said, "I thought we had agreed that your presence in San Sebo would be unwelcome in the future, Mr. Franklin. If the funds for our immigration office had not been held up by the bureaucrats in Whitehall and Washington, I'm not altogether certain the authorities would have permitted you to deplane."

"I apologize for the intrusion, Sarge. I promise I'm not out to make trouble. The fact is that our little boy"—I was grateful Billy wasn't there to hear me refer to him in that manner—"wanted terribly to see San Sebo for himself after hearing my wife and me talk about it. And you know how it is with kids. I thought you wouldn't mind, what with Billy sort of representing the new generation of tourists who'll be coming along in a few short years. I'm sure you understand."

He allowed himself to be mollified; a buck is a buck, no matter whose hand it was in last. Not that he believed me, but he was willing to listen if there was a possibility of shaking a few shekels out of the money tree. "So," he said. "We appreciate your patronage. Are you sure there isn't anything else you'd like to tell me? A courtesy call from a newly arrived tourist, particularly a tourist staying at one of our lesser— though perfectly satisfactory—hotels is sufficiently unusual as to arouse some small doubts in my mind." He smiled grimly. "At least when the tourist is you, Mr. Franklin."

I smiled back. "I've always admired your forthrightness, Sarge, and you're right. There *is* something else." I dug into my back pocket and extracted a folded paper. "And here it is."

He took the paper from my outstretched hand and examined it. "I see. A hospital autopsy report. But this is only a photocopy."

"That's right. In the unlikely event that I meet with any kind of accident on this trip my lawyers will release the original to the press." Tossing off a line about lawyers in the plural sounds much more impressive than a reference to a single legal eagle, the way a passel of vultures is more ominous than one little birdie flopping around by its lonesome. Even if, like me, you don't have any lawyers at all, much less a stableful.

"Let's go for a walk, Mr. Franklin, and talk some more, shall we? The beach is at its best this time of day, and I wouldn't want you to miss a moment of your brief vacation. Who knows? It could be the last chance you'll ever have to visit us." I missed my footing briefly. Sarge looked at me with concern. "Though I sincerely hope not," he said.

We walked down to the beach and began our stroll. "Just ahead," my guide pointed out, "is our newest restaurant, still under construction. They insist on calling it the Sergeant at Arms, though I said that that wasn't necessary."

"Very handsome," I allowed.

"And far up on the horizon you can just see the foundation being laid for a new hotel." He turned toward me and beamed. "They haven't decided on the name as yet, but if all goes well, it'll be open for the tourists in a few short months. I expect it will go well too, and that we'll have the tourists to fill it. If anything should happen, anything go wrong, if the tourists decide to pass our island by, I don't know what we'd do."

He stopped, and put a friendly hand on my shoulder. "And I don't know what my people would do. They're like children when things go wrong. Volatile. Even violent." His hand weighed twenty-three pounds, and I felt it, ounce by every ounce. "Difficult to restrain."

"But Sarge," I said lightly, "I'm positive nothing will go wrong. Why should it? Why should anyone, why should I or anyone else, want to do anything that would cause trouble for this island?"

"Oh, I'm so happy to hear that," my guide responded. "And now, isn't there something else you'd like to talk about? I don't like to burden a tourist, especially a repeat visitor, with my problems. I want our visitors to be happy."

"So do I," I breathed. "Believe me. Well, to begin, I'd like to give you the original of that hospital report."

"But?"

"Precisely. But there's something I'd appreciate in exchange." He said nothing. I went on. "I don't know how to put this delicately, Sarge. May I be blunt?"

"I never expected anything else. I won't take offense. That I can promise."

"Very well. The point is, if this autopsy report got out, if it were said that your hospital deliberately issued a false report, a report that stated a prominent visitor's death had been caused by a massive coronary when it was actually brought on by the administration of barbiturates under mighty peculiar circumstances, it would cast some ugly doubts on your whole medical facility, which I know is very important to you. And it wouldn't do a hell of a lot for the tourist trade, either. Agreed?"

"Agreed," a flat, cold voice responded. "Go on."

"It would be stupid of me to release anything like that. Why should I want to harm the Seboan people? And more selfishly, some Seboan nationals in the States might take it on themselves to seek some sort of retribution. Punish me, you know?"

"I most certainly do. I do indeed."

"Okay then, this is what I want. Sarge, can we sit under that tree there for a bit? This is getting to be too much sun for me, and I've got sand in my shoes."

"Of course. Though sand in the shoes is a lot better than cement around them. That sounds like an old saying, doesn't it?"

"Uh huh." We sprawled on the sand, our backs against a palm tree, Sarge facing one way and I the opposite, a pair of bookends heavily weighted toward his side. "Sarge, what I'm proposing is a trade. I give you the original of the autopsy report and you give me that letter." I felt like an old Bette Davis movie. "I mean that note, the one that was delivered to Mrs. Lamoureux."

"But I thought it was far from certain that this famous note ever existed. And what would I gain from such an exchange, even if it were possible?"

"I'll be honest," I said, lying in my teeth. "We know you

have the note, because Mrs. Randolph Holland has confessed. My government may use it to pressure Mr. Holland on a subject I can't talk about, except that it involves the media he controls, his newspapers and TV stations. But this could scarcely reflect badly on San Sebo, while the other affair, a false autopsy report—well—" I shrugged my shoulders.

"Mrs. Holland said there was a note? But how would Mrs. Holland know?" The man was genuinely perplexed.

"After all, Sarge, she's not sending you money for nothing on a regular basis, now is she?"

"Mrs. Holland sending me money? *Mrs. Holland?*" He began to laugh. "This gets more interesting as we talk about it. Let's go back to Government House." He sprang to his feet and started walking without waiting for me. Pretty spry for a fat boy, was Sarge.

When I caught up he began to talk again. "I assume this involves your CIA." I held my tongue, which may have been the nonverbal equivalent of a fib. "And your Secretary Jo—"

"Please, Sarge, no names. Don't make me lie. But believe me, if you can see your way to cooperating, there'll be some people who'll remember it for a very long time." And that was no lie, even if I did have my fingers crossed.

"I see." He increased his pace and conversation lagged. I had the strong suspicion that Sarge could envisage secret messages, congratulations from the White House, and certainly an increase in financial support from Washington.

When we got back to his office, he threw himself into his chair and opened a locked drawer in the desk. "You can look at this now," he said, "but you cannot take it. Not until I get the original of that autopsy report, plus any copies you may have made. And incidentally, how can I be sure I would be getting all the copies?"

"Because we're not interested in Henry Olds. The other matter is of much greater importance. We're proposing a trade. Everybody gains; nobody loses."

He chewed on that and then announced, "Very well. But you and your wife and child will stay on San Sebo until the trade is completed." He smiled and sat back, pleased with his cleverness. For a moment it looked as if he might start licking his fur in self-satisfaction.

"Fair enough," I replied, though I wasn't altogether convinced Jane and Billy would agree. "Do you think I could get a look at the note now?"

He produced, almost instantly, a copy. Loretta Holland was right about one thing; this was no woman's handwriting. "I'll go even further," he said. "I'll let you speak to the woman who delivered it to the gullible Mrs. Lamoureux." He picked up his phone and issued instructions.

"Thank you. I'd like that. But tell me, how did you find out about this in the first place? You've been pretty much on top of things from the beginning." A little flattery never hurts.

"It was nothing," the man replied, his smug expression belying his words. "The maid who had the note is a good citizen. Law-abiding, you understand. Before she delivered it, she brought it to me and asked what she should do. I told her to go ahead, but to bring it back if she could. I was interested in finding out what would happen."

And if there would be any opportunities for profit, I added to myself. And apparently there had been. Someone, but not Loretta Holland, had been sending money to Sarge to assure that the note would remain buried as permanently as Elizabeth Olds herself.

The woman arrived. She recognized me immediately and looked at Sarge anxiously. He nodded his assent for her to answer my questions. Basically I had only one: "June," I asked, trying to keep my voice all warm and comfy, "who was it gave you this paper to take to the ladies on the picnic?"

After seeking reassurance from Sarge again, she replied timidly, "I don't know who he is, but he was the man who made the television pictures. The man with the fake hair, the funny hair that come down over his face." Her voice rose. "I didn't do nothing wrong! He give me five American dollars. Sarge know that. I come to Sarge and tell him!"

And give him two-fifty, I thought to myself.

"Then I get it back like Sarge told me and give it to him. Okay I go now?"

"Okay you go," Sarge replied. "You're a good girl, June."

She left, moving as rapidly as I had ever seen anyone on the island move before, relief softening her features the way a snowfall softens a barren landscape, her tensed shoulders relaxing. And why not? Being a hotel maid was a cushy job for San Sebo, better than scratching for pennies selling carved coconut shell souvenirs to tourists on the beach. Of course she was a good girl, and of course she had gone right to Sarge to give him his rightful share of those five dollars.

I thought of someone else who hadn't been so good. "Sarge," I said, "let me ask you about something else. That bartender, the one Mrs. Lamoureux complained about. What happened there?"

"Simple. He accused the lady of putting poison in Mr. Henry Olds's drink. She was upset. So was I. Unfortunately there are a few bad people in this world, even in San Sebo."

I could believe it. "But what happened to him? Why did everyone tell me he was long gone from the island?"

"I think that's enough of questions, Mr. Franklin. After I get my hospital report from you, maybe you ask more. Maybe I answer, maybe not. We'll see. You will send for it now?"

"I'll do better than that," I said, reaching into my back pocket. "Here it is, Sarge, signed, sealed, and delivered."

He accepted the paper with a grin, looked at it, and said, "You're a stylish man, Mr. Franklin. Weren't you worried about having this on you while we were talking?"

"Yes," I answered, "I was worried." I failed to add that I had yet another copy stashed away in New York against future need.

He liked that. "And an honest man, too. But no more questions. We've reached an agreement satisfactory to us both. We should stop there. I have my hospital report, you have a copy of the note sent to your Mrs. Lamoureux. Enough."

He was right. After pledging our lifelong brotherhood I made my exit. Sometimes I think I'm loopy, but things like this convince me that the rest of the world is loopier. Back at the bungalow I asked Billy, "Listen, son, do you think sometimes I'm nuts?"

He gave my question serious consideration and then told me, "Yeah, but so's everybody else too."

"You think everybody else is nuttier than me?"

"Nah. Just about the same. You sort of fit in."

The boy meant to be nice, he was trying to tell me I belonged, that in the nut house a nut is normal. But I still wish he had said that if I was crazy as a loon other people were even more so. Even when I win with this kid I lose.

TWENTY-TWO

Back in New York I was upset on several counts. First, I was back in New York, land of the midnight midnight, and never a good idea. New York may be the Big Apple, but it's a plastic one, prettier than the real thing, but dangerously inflammable. And then the stomach roiled at the realization that Loretta Holland had extricated herself from suspicion by calmly pointing me at her dear old friend Kenny Tillson. Finally, I found it impossible to digest the notion that bubbly, bitchy Ken could have been involved in a calculated murder.

I had to find out, somehow, that it wasn't true, evidence from the maid on San Sebo notwithstanding, and the place to start was with that sailboat ride he and Karlla were presumably on during the fateful morning when Dolly got the note and Lizzie got the works.

The TV production department gave me the number of Karlla's agent, and I left a message for her to contact me. "Hey, sweetie," I said when she called, "how'd you like a drink for free?"

"Drinks are never for free for a girl like I," she said, with devastating logic, "especially when the guy calls me 'sweetie.' Let's have the particulars. Sweetie," she added.

"To be more exact, a drink for which I'll pay, while my wife, who will be there, watches over us. She, however, will pay for her own drink. In fact, why don't you come to dinner tonight or tomorrow? I mean if you're not already dated up for the Stork Club like with Cole Porter or something."

"Sounds more and more suspicious. What'll you do with Jane, keep her in the kitchen? And who's my date, you or your kid? He's nearer my age, no?"

"We won't argue that one. How about it?"

"Hold it a sec while I check. Sure. I'd love to. Tonight. Cole's come down with the flu and I'm not talking to Lucius Beebe. The sonofabitch says I stole his gold garters, so I'm free this evening. What time?"

As I've said before, under the fashionable model gloss Karlla was a solid citizen. She showed up a proper twenty minutes after the time we set, and she was porting a bottle of Mumm's. "I usually bathe in this stuff," she announced, "but I figured you might enjoy a change from your Dr. Pepper."

"I wouldn't want to deprive you," I said. "I'll climb in the tub with you."

"So," Jane said ominously, "will I."

"I'll eat," my practical stepson assured us. "I'll leave you all the green vegetables."

Mindful of the iron discipline that top flight models practice, we had planned a reasonably low calorie dinner—swordfish broiled with lemon juice and herbs in place of butter, green beans dressed with seasoned vinegar, as was the salad, and dessert an apple, plus, to be deliciously sinful, a teensy wedge of cheddar. We had Karlla's champagne, but what the hell, as the girl herself said, she could always run up and down the stairs half a dozen times to work it off.

After dinner Billy left for the homework shift in his bedroom, and the ladies and I huddled around our coffee (no cream) and got down to serious business. "Karlla," I began, "this San Sebo affair with Elizabeth Olds won't quiet down. It keeps raising its nasty little head and throwing suspicions up in the air to see who gets dirty."

"That's Lizzie Olds for you," Karlla said. "Out to clobber somebody with her last breath plus six months. What's your problem now, son?"

"It turns out that there really was a phony note somebody sent so they could get her by herself. You can see what that could mean. So we've all got to be sure again of our alibis. I hate to use dramatic words like that, but that's what it comes down to."

Karlla looked annoyed. Jane jumped in. "Of course you and Kenny are in the best spot of all of us, being out on that boat. That's what Ev means; he only wants to double check everyone's story to get it all straight in case there's trouble. God knows what that nut who runs the island could get up to if he puts his mind to it. We're talking to everybody," she concluded, with pardonable exaggeration.

"Oh, I guess so," Karlla said with an exasperated sigh. "What do you want to know, the whole story all over again?"

"I'm afraid so. And with as much detail as you can give us."

She composed her thoughts quietly for a moment. "Okay. Give me another smidge of coffee, if there's any in the pot, will you?" Frowning thoughtfully, she watched the coffee being poured. "That's enough. That's fine." She sipped a bit. "Well. Kenny and I met about nine that morning. The production crew didn't expect to be ready to start shooting the next commercial until late afternoon, so we had arranged for this sailboat. We took off from the harbor maybe nine-thirty or so with a couple of sandwiches, a six-pack of beer for him and some diet shit for me. When we got back all hell had broken loose with the Lamoureux woman and Lizzie Olds, everybody was hooting it up in the hotel lobby, and that's where you found us. I don't think we had been there for even an hour when you saw us. So what can I tell you?"

"I don't know," I admitted.

"Where'd you go sailing?" Jane asked.

Karlla looked blank. "How the hell do I know? We just went sailing. Around the island. I know we got to the lagoon on the other side from the harbor, because that's where Ken decided to drop anchor and go swimming."

Jane and I traded quick glances; the lagoon opposite the harbor side of the island was where the two women had been picnicking. "How long were you anchored there?" I asked.

"Too damn long," Karlla said bitterly. "That's how I got the sunburn. If I'd known how to sail the fool boat I would have left Ken there to swim forever if he wanted, but I didn't. Believe me, I was that mad I could've dropped anchor on him if I'd had half a chance. Anyway, it must have been nearer to an hour than a half hour before he got back, and then he had to muck around sailing into the wind because he didn't know any more about sailing than I did." She snorted. "He said he was tacking, that that was the way to do it, but it looked to me a couple of times like we were headed for Portugal. That didn't help the sunburn either, I can tell you."

She looked up. "Don't get me wrong, though. I still love the stupid bastard. I'd just like to slit his throat a little."

"Definition of love," Jane said. "I know what you mean."

"And," I added, "from personal experience let me say that I know she knows what you mean. Many's the time I've been grateful my shirt collar hid my neck at the office."

"That why you wear those oldie timie high collars? I always thought you were trying to look like Herbert Hoover," Karlla said. "I thought it was cute. Anyway," she added, getting serious again, "I don't know what else I can tell you, do you?"

She had, of course, told us enough. More than enough. Enough to make a body wonder about what else was under

Kenny's wig besides a happy face. The next step was to find out.

I called Ken at the office the next day and made a lunch date. "I'll spring for it," I said, "and stick *Glo and Get It* with the tab."

"Hey," he said, "we ought to ring Karlla in on that. She gave those finks good value for their money. See what's happening to their sales since the new campaign got going?"

"No. This is strictly stag." It was going to be tough enough poking around to see if I could stick Ken Tillson with a dollop of guilt without having Karlla around to observe how I had used her. "Besides, whatever made the product sell it wasn't your commercials."

"That's an effing crock, sweetheart. What do you mean?"

"Exactly what I said. We had a closed circuit test. Two months of it. The market is just as hot for Clairol as it ever was, whether you shovel *Glo* commercials at it or not."

"You're putting me on."

"Unh unh, I'm not. I'll tell you about it at lunch. But no Karlla." I wasn't putting him on, either. There's a couple of towns in the country where lots of homes are hooked into a closed circuit TV system and the residents have been convinced that it would be unAmerican of them to refuse to keep a diary of their purchases over a period of weeks or months. Then, without their knowing that they're being experimented on like the hapless victims in a mad scientist's dungeon, half of them are tortured by commercials for a brand we're interested in, in this case *Glo and Get It,* while the other half get anything else that happens to be on hand—headache remedies, dog food, Japanese cars, whatever. It all comes over the air as if it were normal television fare, and all on the same regularly scheduled programs.

Then we collect the diaries and see if there's been any measurable effect, meaning did the viewers who saw our commercials rev up their purchases any more than those who weren't exposed.

They didn't, in this case. Which increased both my admiration and respect for the American woman for deciding that a beautiful model galloping in soft focus and trailing a quarter of a mile of chiffon had little if anything to do with the effectiveness of the hair coloring she was pushing. I'd tell you the names of a couple of the towns that are hooked into such systems, but somebody might hit me if I did. And kick me in the pocketbook, which is worse. Anyway, I wasn't lying to Kenny and I managed to achieve my goal of not inviting Karlla, and if an ad man can achieve his goal without either lying or at least stretching the truth unbearably, he's practically a candidate for sainthood, which may be why no ad man has ever been canonized, as far as I have been able to ascertain.

We met at lunch. Despite my telling Kenny this was strictly stag I brought Jane because she's much shrewder than I am at thinking up sneaky lines of questioning. I started with the same patter we had used on Karlla about having to doublecheck everybody's alibi.

"What a bore," Ken said. "Anyway, you know my story. It's short and sweet, just like me, dolly. Karlla and I were out on a boat the whole time the stuff was hitting the fan. We got back for the third act, when you rescued the virtuous maiden from the villain. What's to say, other than that?"

"What about the note you wrote Dolly Lamoureux?" I asked.

"What about it? I'd never write that broad. Hell, she's fatter than I am."

"Cut the comedy, Ken. Your friend Loretta told us about it."

"You're kidding! No, scratch that. You're fishing, Ev, and I don't know what for. I don't think the food here is that good, for you to try working some kind of an act on me. Now really!"

Jane is good at unruffling feathers. "Kenny," she said, "it's the other way around. Ev is trying to get at the truth because it looks more and more as if the Olds woman was murdered, and if anybody wants to say that you were responsible—hell, we don't want to sit and wait for trouble—we want to head it off at the pass. The thing is, maybe you and Loretta Holland were kids together, but she's a different pussycat now, and her concern is Loretta Holland, great lady and head honcho. She even gave us a copy of the note. Lord knows where she got it, but she gave it to us, and what's more, she said it's in your handwriting. So please, Kenny, help. Please help."

It was the first time I had ever seen pain and confusion on the man's face, and I hoped it would be the last time. He looked from one of us to the other, mouth agape, starting to form words only to find that nothing wanted to come out, which was another first. Finally, a gentle "I don't believe it," issued forth.

"I'm sorry, Ken," I said, reaching into a pocket and unfolding a copy of the copy. "Here it is, just as la Holland gave it to us. You wrote it, didn't you?"

He said nothing. He looked at his plate as if it had betrayed him, as if the food had turned to pasteboard models purely out of malice. Jane put her hand on his and said, "Please, Kenny, don't make us check. Tell us if you wrote it, just tell us yes or no."

A tear trickled down his cheek, catching in the groove alongside his mouth that had been dug by laughter what seemed now like a thousand years ago. "Loretta's an old buddy. How could she have done this to me? I don't understand." He looked down at his hands resting on the table like alien objects that might do something else of their own volition that once again couldn't be explained.

"Tell us what happened, Kenny," Jane said softly.

"No, not here. Not with all the damned food around." He looked at us with his face contorted into an unconvincing imitation of his famous wicked grin. "If I tell you here it might curdle the cream sauce, darlings, and we wouldn't want that, would we, not at these prices! Let's go up to your office or someplace. Someplace quiet."

We went to my office. Ken sat in the cushioned visitor's chair, Jane and I on the couch. I asked Sally to get us some coffee, black, and when she had, I opened a cabinet drawer and drew out a bottle of cognac. "Forget you saw this, you two," I said as I splashed some into Kenny's cup. "This is my own little secret."

"Fair enough," Ken said. "Now I'll tell you mine." It hurt to see the man force himself into a jaunty smile. "And believe me, sweetheart, it makes yours look feeble. You always were a rectangle, Franklin." He explained to Jane: "That's half a square, dear.

"Well, I wrote that note. Indeedy, yes. Loretta—my old friend Loretta—said she couldn't get away from Randy until noon and she had to see the Olds woman alone. She knew about the picnic plans the two old girls had, and she told me what to write, and to get someone from the hotel to deliver it to the Lamoureuxs. It sounded a little tacky, but what the hell, Loretta was a buddy." He fell into silence as he contemplated what Loretta was then, and what she was now.

"Anyway, Karlla and I had our own plans for the boat, so I got one of the maids before we left, maybe nine o'clock that morning. I slipped her five bucks and told her there'd be five more if she delivered the cursed thing a little after twelve. She did, as you well know. And then she took it to that awful darkie who runs the joint, as I certainly didn't well know. And the next thing was your Mr. Sarge shuffling around and suggesting that while he was certain I hadn't done anything wrong, various other unnamed parties might not agree, and in order to make assurance doubly sure I might like to make a small but regular contribution to his favorite charity, himself. Nothing immodest. Something like fifty bucks a month. A bargain, he assured me. Can you imagine!"

"You've actually been paying Sarge all this time? I can't believe it!" I said.

"Oh, hell, no. I refused on the spot, of course. He told me to think it over. I didn't have to think it over, and I told Loretta what the nervy twit had wanted. She agreed I was absolutely right, but that the ugly bastard could cause all sorts of upset, and she said she'd send it to him, that I should tell him he'd be getting it in cash in the mail but that after a year it would stop. I'll say that for him, when it comes to blackmail, he thinks small. What the hell, Loretta could take it out of her Fabergé egg money, I suppose, and never even miss it. And after all, I expect he could have caused trouble if he'd had a mind to."

"Did Loretta say why she wanted to get Lizzie Olds off by herself?" I asked.

"Yeah, and it was an absolutely stinking idea. She thought, quite wrongly, that she could convince the old girl to sell out, because the Olds outfit wasn't going to be anything Lizzie could run herself, and the Hollands thought they needed it to keep their own little ship from sinking. She thought maybe an appeal to the heart, as if there was a heart somewhere inside that ample bosom instead of only a couple more layers of ample bosom. Why," he exclaimed, with another try at being jaunty, "it was just a Japanese puzzle of a bosom, ample bosom within ample bosom within ditto until it ended up with a microchip at the center keeping the old girl running and behaving almost like a real flesh and blood human being, almost."

"Did Loretta and Lizzie fight? Did she tell you about that?"

He shook his head. "Not so's I know anything. She said the old lady wouldn't even talk to her. Just walked away."

"What about the knitting needle?"

Bafflement set in. "Knitting needle? What do you mean? Honeybunch, I wouldn't know a knitting needle from an Australian nose pick. What about a knitting needle? If you're planning on making me argyle socks for Christmas, forget it; it's been twenty years since I've had a hankering to look like a plastic Princeton boy."

Kenny could have been lying; he'd been around actors long enough to have picked up some of the tricks. I had to try something else. "Look, Kenny, don't jump down my throat, but when you were out on the boat—I don't know how to put this, because I guess I tricked Karlla into telling me—she didn't intentionally try to pin anything on you—it was just that, well, I don't know exactly—"

"For heaven's sake, stop blathering, Franklin! Out with it. I've been practicing Marie Antoinette mounting the guillotine with grace and breeding every night for the last three decades, so I can take it." He looked thoughtful. "Though if you give me enough time to brood I might start asking why the devil I *should* take it. So get to it, junior, before I doze off, will you?"

"Okay. Karlla says you went for a long, long swim while you were around the back of the island on the boat. She says that's why she was stuck there broiling in the sun. You were off paddling in the surf. And that couldn't have been far from where the ladies were picnicking. You could've gone ashore there, and—well, you know."

"No, I don't know, you nit, and neither do you. Listen to me, Franklin. Once and for all." Ken had been going green and yellow alternately as he contemplated Loretta Holland's perfidy, but now he turned a bright red, an apoplectic parallel to an English peaches and cream complexion, a sort of raw beef and peanut oil. "Yes, I could've gone ashore there, and no, I don't know. My old granny used to talk about people not having any gumption these days. She should've known you, you nervy sonofa!" He bristled, indignant as a duchess.

Jane got in the act. "Now wait a minute, Kenny. You're not angry with Ev, and you know it. It's Loretta Holland who's dumped on you, isn't it? If Ev doesn't ask you these questions you can be damn sure somebody else will. A cop, and not the Keystone variety like friend Sarge. So swallow hard and pull yourself together. And let's have an answer."

"That's great for you to say, puss, but how'd you like it if it was your ass on the line?"

"Think hard," Jane said, very evenly. "If Ev and I thought you had done anything to the Olds woman, do you think we'd be sitting here asking you about it? If I really thought you'd gone after her like that I wouldn't even get in the opposite end of a crowded subway car from you. Use your head. Simmer down."

He sat back; the beefsteak faded to rosy red, though a suspicion of peanut oil lingered on. He favored me with one last resentful glare, and said, "Okay. Okay, but watch it, is all I've got to say. As it happens, I did start to swim to shore, simply to have a point to aim at, so I could figure out where I was headed instead of going in circles, like some people I could name." He leveled an accusing eye at me. "But it was too far. I couldn't make it. The current kept carrying me further down the beach."

I must have put on a skeptical expression because he snapped. "No, I'm not going to say I was swept out to sea and drowned, Franklin, because, and I can prove it by sinking my teeth into your jugular, I wasn't. But I did hitch a ride back to the boat from some fishermen. They picked me up all hell and gone down to the east end of the island and ferried me back to Karlla. Didn't the silly bitch tell you that too? Or did she only remember the unimportant things like me breaststroking my way toward Lizzie Olds with a cavalry saber between my teeth? And I'll bet I could prove it if I had to, which I don't, in my own opinion."

He leaned forward and leered in my direction. "You know why?"

"No, but I'd like to," I said as modestly as I could.

"Because I gave the boys who took me back to the boat my beer, the whole damn six-pack, which probably represented about as much money as they'd have made fishing more than half a day. From the noise they made, maybe even more. And I threw in a couple of cans of the sugar-free slops Karlla had wagged along." He snorted. "If I'd known what was going to happen I would have thrown her in too. They'll remember me, if anybody wants to check, and they can tell you how they found me wallowing like a mothering whale out there in the deep." He folded his arms across his chest in self-righteous triumph.

"Oh, Kenny," Jane lied, "we knew you'd be able to tell us something like that. I'm just delighted. Delighted and relieved."

"How about that one?" Ken asked, jerking his head in my direction. "He delighted, too?"

"Yeah," I said, "just delighted."

"How 'bout relieved. You relieved?"

"Can you doubt it?" I asked, just a tap sullenly.

"If I work at it a little. Uh huh, I can doubt it." With that he stood, posed regally, and marched out under his wig as if it were the Russian Imperial Crown.

After he shut the door behind him, and none too gently, I turned to Jane. "You think I lost a friend?"

"Maybe, maybe not. But these things even out. You lose a friend, you gain an enemy. So relax. Take it easy. It'll all go away after a bit."

TWENTY-THREE

We went upstate to the cottage that weekend, Jane, Billy, and I. Woodstock had decided to be crisp and cold, just the weather that calls for hot mulled wine. While I prepared the brew for Jane and me and Jane heated Billy a mug of cocoa, we talked about Loretta Holland and Ken Tillson as alternate candidates for murderer. "We know Kenny wrote the note," I said, "and that he could've swum over to Lizzie Olds at that picnic no matter what he says about jolly fishermen sweeping him up in their nets."

"Yes," Jane agreed, "but Loretta said something to you about knitting needles, which she couldn't have known about if she hadn't been on the scene."

"Unless your buddy Ken Tillson told her about it," Billy pointed out.

"But he says he didn't know about the knitting needle."

"Yeah," Billy said, "he *says* he didn't know about it. You gonna believe him? Far as that goes, you gonna believe her?"

"So what've we got?" I asked plaintively.

Silence. Then the boy spoke up. "I'll tell you what you got. You got mulled wine. I don't got mulled wine. I got cocoa, for God's sake! I'm going on fifteen and I got cocoa."

"That's right," his mother affirmed. "When you're older you'll get mulled wine."

"Aw, ma, cocoa's bad for the teeth. All that sugar. Yech!"

"Uh huh, and wine's bad for the liver. All that alcohol. Yech!"

"That's different, ma."

I kept quiet. In some ways I knew the boy better than his mother did, having been worsted by him a myriad of times in adversary tangles. I watched, fascinated to see how he'd bring this one off.

"Okay," Jane said with a sigh, "tell me about it. How's it different?"

"It's different on account of if your liver rots no one can see it, but if it's your teeth you look like hell and I'm too young for that. You want me to look like Ev before I'm even twenty? I'll never get a date, all this lousy cocoa, ma."

I felt compassion, not for the suffering child but for my wife's head, which she had just placed in the noose her son had arranged for her. "Jane," I said, "he's almost right. And look, there's water in the wine, and some of the alcohol has to have boiled away when I heated it." I omitted the fact that mulled wine has sugar in it too, because when it came to his wanting that first swig of hooch my sympathies were with Billy. "He's old enough. Let him try it."

Jane frowned. Billy looked expectant, but he was shrewd enough to hold his tongue. "Okay," Jane announced. "Not a lot, but okay. Just enough to start you down the primrose path, boy, but if you end up on the Bowery, don't try to con half a buck out of your old mother."

"Thanks, ma. You too, Ev, thanks a lot." He poured himself an inch into a coffee mug while Jane stood watch. He sipped, licked his lips, sipped again. "You know what, ma," he said, "I think maybe I'll have a Coke instead. This stuff is—I dunno."

"Yech?" I suggested.

"That's about it," he agreed, "but thanks anyway."

We regrouped around the fireplace. "To go back," I said, "what've we got?"

"Well," Jane said tentatively, "we agreed that if Lizzie Olds was murdered then the same person did in Henry as well. Loretta had the chance, God knows, what with all those drinks she and Dolly were fixing the man. And she told you she had been a nurse, didn't she?"

"In training for a nurse," I said, "before she went into modeling. But heck, I doubt if she'd be wagging around a pound and a half of anything called pentobarbitol sodium in case she met up with someone she wanted to knock off. And how would she get it in San Sebo, for heaven's sake?"

That murdered Billy. "I like that, Ev! My good man," he said in a high, affected voice, "kindly have the pharmacist delivah seventeen and a hahhf grains of your veddy finest pentosodapoppy to my suite eemedjately or I shall have your head separated from your torso, not to mention vice-uh ver-suh." He cackled happily.

I ignored the interruption. "And anyway, Kenny was there too, remember. Talking to Loretta. If he wanted to poison the old man, he could have done it. If nobody saw him fiddle with a drink—well, he wouldn't have wanted anyone to see him, would he?"

"Maybe they were in it together," Jane suggested halfheart-edly.

"It's a thought," I said, "and even a possibility. And listen, we figured it was the same one dispatched both the Oldses, but maybe not. Dolly Lamoureux's still a little bit on the hook, for my money. At least in Henry's case."

"Gee," Billy said, boredom in his voice, "you two are going to kick this around forever, just sitting here. When you going to do something, 'stead of only talking?"

"Like what, wise guy?" I asked.

"Well, you're going to see all these jokers again in Pebble

Beach pretty soon, aren't you? Why don't you see what you can think of, go after them. You know."

"I don't know. Not really, but it's a thought."

"Just one thing, Ev. When you're out there with them, re-member, one of them could be a killer. Maybe two." My stepson's eyes glittered. "You better be careful."

"I've been brooding about that already, son, but thanks."

"'at's okay. Just watch your ass—"

"Billy!" (Jane, firmly.)

"—paragus. Aw, ma!"

And my back and my jugular and my health in general, it occurred to me. And my asparagus as well, as Billy would have it.

□

TWENTY-FOUR

□

It was time to get ready for Pebble Beach. I had to see that my regular work at the office got done as well, and, if I wanted, I had to prepare myself for the extracurricular sleuthing I might find myself involved in out on the Coast.

The first was easy. As I've said, as a species board members are to a man firm believers in the restorative powers of sleep, especially as practiced during meetings, so it didn't matter all that much what I told them as long as I told it to them with firmness and authority and backed up my blather with charts and numbers. I shouldn't make it sound too easy, though, because there's an art to it. To begin with, there has to be an array of slick, colorful charts and illustrations to show how professional we at Finch, etc., are at preparing ourselves for these oh-so-important conclaves. But to this needs to be added at least a handful of what look like hastily scribbled charts done with magic marker pens. These latter demonstrate that our team isn't out to snow the board with a lot of artistic gimmickry, but that our main effort is to give them all the facts they need to judge our plans for the coming year, even when those facts are so new that there's no time to gussy them up with fancy art work. A boy needs to be experienced to strike the proper balance between the two approaches, and I had it, though I say so myself.

I divided my material into two piles and got together with the art director. "Listen," I explained, "these here are for slick production. Give me one of your crew to work with and I'll tell him what I'm after. And these," I added, giving him the second batch, "make up like last-minute stuff. And remember, you've only got ten days to get it all ready."

"No problem," he said, "so long as you don't keep changing things after we've got it done." I ignored him, though he was right. Part of the act of being a Big Executive is to know everybody else's work better than they do, and to tell them all about it. But that's another story, and I'm not going to criticize myself. After all, everybody one-ups the next guy, so why shouldn't I?

The second problem was taking care of the day-to-day office work mushrooming in the in-box. The only immediate difficulty was with the prophylactics client. Their sales had been falling off, and they wanted to know why. They had written a letter to the agency, and, as it always does, the letter had ultimately been shunted to the research department with a note from Ed Jorgensen: "Pl. answer instanter for my signature. Note date of receipt." I noted date of receipt; it had been in the house nearly two weeks before they were considerate enough to think of dumping it on me.

The cursed thing was from their marketing man, a pixie whose very existence was an argument for birth control. He included a clipping from a medical journal claiming that male joggers experienced an enormous drop in the levels of testosterone after their favorite exercise, and engaged in sexual congress with their loved one or ones only half as often as previously. He wanted to know if we thought that the popularity of jogging was a factor in their declining sales, and if so, whether they should consider an anti-jogging campaign, giving whatever evidence there was about it being bad for the heart, the knees, the lungs, and naturally for all those absolutely bushed sperm cells. Maybe, he concluded, people were eschewing sex for more serious forms of exercise.

I thought of many answers, few of them polite. I solved the problem with another Big Executive decision by calling in Joe Harris, my first assistant. "Joe," I said, "prepare me an answer to this thing, and let me have it this afternoon." I watched his face dissolve with dismay as he read what I had handed him. "Don't worry about it. Just waltz the guy around. Jolly him up. You can do it." I was getting to sound like Jorgensen.

A few other items of office work and I could think about the third problem area, how and what, if anything, to do about bloodhounding it in Pebble Beach. A few hours of brooding, self-analysis, soul searching, and chewing the erasers off pencils, and I was able to arrive at a firm conclusion: There was absolutely nothing I could do in advance about Pebble Beach. However, in advertising we never admit defeat, even to ourselves, which means that rather than tell myself I was stymied, I announced to the inner man that the wisest thing to do would be to play it by ear. See what happens. Don't pin yourself down with too much forward planning, boy. Be young, alert, dance lightly on the balls of your feet, and watch out, Loretta Holland et al., here I come! That's what we call image-building on Madison Avenue, or how to make a mover and shaker out of a tired middle-aged man with a creeping waistline.

There was one other development that day. Joe Harris outmaneuvered me by sticking his face in and saying, "Ev, about this contraceptive thing you asked me to look into."

"Right. You finished? Got a draft I can see?"

"Not really."

"Whaddya mean, not really. Is it yes or is it no?"

"I'm afraid it's no. I can't work on it."

"For God's sake, why not? It can't be all that difficult."

"It's not the difficulty, Ev. You're right about that. For God's sake, that's exactly why not, that's why I can't work on it."

"What in the name of Margaret Sanger are you talking about?"

"Well, Ev, you know how Jane refused to work on the cigarette account? She said it was a matter of conscience?"

"So?"

"It's the same thing with the prophylactic account for me. You know I'm Catholic, Ev, and I can't work on this. I just can't. It's against my religious convictions. I'm sorry."

Oh, that devil. Maybe he was Catholic and then again maybe he had whipped over to St. Patrick's during lunch hour and been converted. All I knew was two things: Joe Harris didn't have the religious convictions of a stuffed cabbage, and whether he did or didn't, he had me, in spades. I couldn't argue about his declining an assignment as a matter of conscience. It wasn't done. I'd have to do it myself. Outfoxed. Foiled again. It served me right for trying to emulate a top executive by hanging a tiresome problem around somebody else's neck.

I finally squeezed out a reply for Jorgensen's signature, saying that we had discussed the matter with the agency's consultant on religious affairs, a position I invented for the occasion, and that he had cautioned us to lay low on the subject of jogging and testosterone. I said his opinion was that few people would have read the obscure medical journal, but that if the client started bad-mouthing jogging we'd end up giving the theory greater currency, turn the company into a branch of the Great Satan, and clog every highway in the country with able-bodied men jogging for population control. The things I'm forced to do for a living.

The next day I got back the carbon of the letter, which Jorgensen had signed and sent out. He had written "GREAT!" on my copy. That meant he hadn't read it but had observed that it was lengthy enough to look as if he had given the matter very careful thought, which is all agency presidents care about.

Thus stimulated by praise from my betters, I took another stab at wondering about my Pebble Beach problem. This time I got somewhere. For one thing, I remembered something else that had happened on San Sebo, something I hadn't connected up with all the deliberate mayhem; and it occurred to me that if Loretta Holland had had anything to do with it and with the two murders I might be able to psych her out. That evening at home I cut out the brand name from a package, put it in an envelope, and printed a note saying, "Madam: You were seen. Please remit $1,000 as soon as possible. Do not force me to let the inquisitive Mr. Franklin know about this." I signed the note "Sarge."

But I started brooding that she might actually send the money, and I saw no reason to arrange for out of season Christmas presents to be delivered to that tub of guts, so I reopened the envelope and changed the request to a slightly larger one, for a million bucks. That, I was almost certain, might be a shade too much for Loretta Holland to have on hand, even if she asked her hubby for money to go to the powder room at The Quilted Giraffe two or three times an evening.

I was late to work the next day because I stopped off at the Seboan mission to the U.N. before hitting the office. By flashing two crackling new fifties I was able to convince a young person to accept one of them as partial payment for the note to be shipped to San Sebo and then sent out again with a Seboan postmark on it. The second fifty would be handed over when my girlfriend down on Gramercy Park got delivery. It was that easy, and I was reasonably certain that care would be taken to keep Sarge from snooping into this one. Even if he did, he'd never have been able to puzzle through the gimmick.

Now at last I knew I'd have Loretta Holland on the run. If she was a murderer. If she wasn't, she'd ignore the polite request from Sarge and figure the tropic sun had melted the man's brain. I could hardly wait—hardly wait to get back from Pebble Beach alive, that is. I wished I had done detective story things like buy the notepaper I wrote on somewhere out of my neighborhood, like Bayonne, New Jersey, wipe fingerprints off everything, wear gloves while I was carrying it around, destroy the gloves afterwards so nobody could prove that the hair in the letter was actually from the fur lining in the demented Everett Franklin's mittens, etc. But the gloves were a present from Jane, so the devil with it, I figured, I'll take my chances. Anyway, it was too late now. The brakes were off and the juggernaut was rolling.

□
TWENTY-FIVE
□

Thursday evening, just short of two weeks later, Jane and I left for Pebble Beach. Once again I would be arriving in advance of the board to inspect the arrangements at the hotel, inevitably canceling half of them for having been incorrectly prepared, and larding the hotel staff with gold as apology for my impudence in asking them to let us have what we had contracted for.

My mind wasn't on the job, however; I was too busy stewing about Loretta Holland's reactions to the letter purportedly from Sarge that she would have had for over a week by now. The only certainty was that she wouldn't have sent Sarge a million bucks, guilty or innocent. At one point I wasn't even completely sure about that. I had a midnight vision of the lady drawling casually to her husband, "Oh, by the way, Randy, ducks, do you mind if I go through your wallet tonight and take out a spare mil? There's this diamond I picked up from Harry Winston and I simply didn't have enough change in my reticule. Thank you, dear, and do remember to take it out of my allowance next week, you old pussycat."

I needn't have worried about not giving the arrangements the full benefit of my critical eye. These affairs have a life of their own, and once the start button is pushed they lumber forward whether the machinery is checked and oiled or not, like aging chorus girls going through their high kicks in spite of aching joints so they can get it over with, slip out of their tight shoes, and relax. Forget the machinery, if you must, as long as the big brass is adequately oiled; I did see to it that the bar was properly stocked.

The meeting was the same and yet different from the previous one. The Hollands and the Lamoureuxs were present, as was Dorothy Braun. Early on, Dolly Lamoureux observed, "Poor Henry and Elizabeth. We'll miss them, won't we?" Nobody answered, of course, though a few faces looked ready to observe that absence makes the heart grow forgetful, fatuous, and phony.

The difference was in part the presence of new board members, the usual assortment of tycoons, moguls, and pukka sahibs, and one temporary appointment, that of Henry Olds's nephew Albert Biedermeier, or, as he was informally (and patronizingly) dubbed, Allie Biedermeier. Allie had been granted the post until a new election could be held, as a gesture to honor the deceased Henry, and also because he appeared eminently ignorable. But more significant in making this meeting different was the absence of the heavy hands of the Oldses. No Henry to make others dangle above a slow fire of his devising, and no Elizabeth to shed the grace of total disapproval over the assemblage.

There was a big turnout on Friday evening, the usual convivial get-together before the major event on Saturday. Even Holland's pilot had been invited, Randolph saying grandly that he knew we'd all want to meet the hero whose quick thinking had saved Mr. and Mrs. Franklin as well as Mrs. Olds from a watery grave. With his usual delicacy he blithely skipped over the fact, which had to have been damned near engraved in Day-Glo colors on the minds of everyone present, that at least one of those saved had managed to make it more successfully into a second watery grave shortly thereafter, without the interference of Holland's hired hand.

Despite the glare of disapproval from Ed Jorgensen, I spent my first fifteen minutes not jollying up my betters but with the pilot; he had, after all, managed to get us out safely, and the last I had seen of him had been through a screen of seaweed and worse in the island paradise harbor. I thanked him and asked if he had sustained any permanent damage.

"Oh, no. I'm fine. We were all lucky. Though the Hollands keep treating me as if parts were going to drop off. Especially Mrs. Holland."

"Mrs. Holland?" This was a new and oddly different Loretta, showing concern for someone else for more than a split second, especially when nobody was going to alert *The New York Times*.

"Damn right. Even coming out here she did as much piloting as I did. Insisted on it. Made me go back and lie down. Good pilot, too, she is. Would you believe? She even sent me on vacation, all expenses paid, after I got on my feet again. And there wasn't nothing much wrong with me! She don't just look like a doll; she *is* a doll, I tell ya."

"That's terrific," I said. "Tell me, though, did they ever find out what the trouble with the plane was, what went wrong? What really happened to us, you know?"

"Something with the fuel line, I don't know what. You'd have to ask Mrs. H about it. She got the report while I was on that vacation. Jeez, was that terrific! You know she sent me and my old lady to the best damn hotels I ever was in, down on the Riviera. If I wasn't sick before I got there I woulda been from all that eating we did. Makes a guy want to be rich. Anyway, you want to know, she can tell you. Knows damn near as much as me about planes."

I figured he'd say something like that; I was sure I had hit the jackpot.

Ed Jorgensen came over and joined us. Very briefly. Long

enough to say to the pilot, "Good to see you back with us," and then turn to me to mutter, "Listen, mix it up with the board, will you, Franklin! That's what you're here for, no?"

"I was wondering what I was here for, Ed. Okay, so I'll mix." I wandered over to where Randolph Holland was laughing raucously in a little group of one of the new boys, Dolly Lamoureux, and Dorothy Braun. He looked happy, as well he might, since he had none of the worries that were on him at the last meeting, including Henry Olds. Dolly looked passionately interested in the manner of a lady trying desperately to look passionately interested when she'd rather have been home chatting it up with her petunias. Dorothy Braun looked irritated and slightly overloaded with drink. The new boy, a banker, looked unconvinced in general banker style.

"Hey, there, boy," Holland bawled, "I was just telling the girls here about truth in advertising. You know how our Dorothy is about that. Real sincere. Anyway, I was talking about those ads that keep bugling how thisa and thata is only pennies a day, only pennies a day, and before you know it you go broke pennyadaying it to some Shylock of a banker." The banker appeared as annoyed as Ms. Braun.

Holland warmed up to his subject. "Yeah, and this bull about one product gives you less radiation than a dentist's X ray and another gives you even less radiation, and everything's hunky-dory until you get undressed one night and turn out the light and your dong is glowing in the dark like a neon salami. You know what I mean?" He looked at Dorothy Braun and leered, daring her to be offended.

Fortunately she was drunk enough to rise to the challenge. She swigged a mouthful of what looked terribly much like gin on the rocks. "Neon gherkin, you mean," she said coolly.

Holland stopped short. "Huh?"

"I said you look down at a neon gherkin, not a salami." She smiled, the sweetest smile I had ever seen on a lady dean, drunk or sober. "As in itty bitty pickle. You know how I am about truth in advertising, Randy." She grabbed my arm to steady herself, and led me away. "I loathe that uncouth prick," she confided.

I nearly kissed her. "Well, you needn't. I think you've struck a blow for the common man. A mortal blow, I'd say." I took her to a table and sat her down to regroup, while I headed out again.

Loretta was seated in an easy chair at the side of the reception room, a gaggle of men around her, all standing. She looked at me and nodded, simultaneously lifting a cigarette to her lips. She neither asked for a light nor looked at the man supplying it. She merely accepted it as something which she had willed into existence, as part of the tribute owed to her by the world. It struck me more forcefully than ever that Loretta Holland was a woman who would insist that the world come to her with no reciprocal gestures on her part, but that once it had arrived she would much prefer that it wait outside in the rain if such positioning suited her convenience.

If she had received the blackmail note she showed no sign of it.

I went over and joined the group, met the new corporation lawyer on our board, smiled at one at all, and ended up separating from the others with one of the worshipers, who happened to be Allie Biedermeier. As we moved off, Loretta said, "Oh, dear, Mr. Franklin, and I was so sure you'd come for a talk with me. I'm devastated."

"We'll be talking later," I said. "You can count on it. A trip to the Coast wouldn't be complete without it."

"I'll be waiting. And ready."

I got Allie off in a quiet corner. I could see Ed Jorgensen on the other side of the room frowning, and I realized that he had elected Albert Biedermeier, Esq., as the board member with the lowest priority for waltzing around, since his appointment was a temporary expedient. After all, why waste courtesies on someone who'd be gone in a couple of months and was therefore the most easily dismissed among all those present? I turned slightly so that Ed's frown bounced off my shoulder, leaving only the slightest of burn marks. "I'm glad we've finally met," I said to Allie. "Your aunt and uncle often talked about you."

The man did a double take. "They talked about me? And

168

you still wanted to meet me?" He laughed. "You know I'm not here because I was Uncle Henry's favorite nephew. I'm here because I was his only nephew. He didn't leave me everything; he just not left it to anybody else, that's all." He laughed again. "If he could see me now at this board meeting, it'd kill him even deader." He raised his glass in a happy toast to Uncle.

Allie may not have inherited his uncle's brains but the two boys were of a piece when it came to family feeling. "I gather yours was not a particularly close family relationship," I said, grinning.

"You can say that again. In a way, though, I admired the old bastard. He liked life and he lived a lot of it. On the other hand, Aunt Lizzie—she hated anyone calling her Lizzie— Aunt Elizabeth lived a lot of life and enjoyed hating every minute of it. I can't blame her too much, I guess, not with the way Henry catted around for most of his seventy-odd years. Very odd years," he added. "Except for money, and I suppose power, that's what he thought of most, sex. Sex without Aunt Lizzie, you understand."

Something made him smile broadly. "You know what he said one time, the old goat?" I shook my head, though I would have given odds that it was something wicked that involved both sex and Elizabeth. I was right. "He said that after the first fifty years sixty-nine is a position you get into when you and your wife want to hold ice to each other's piles." This time he didn't laugh. He brayed.

I was tired of Henry's sex life. Karlla had already given me a lifetime supply of the man's aphorisms on the subject. But there were some things I did want to hear about. "Still, it's sad," I said, without specifying precisely what it was that was sad. "They were both so very much alive. Tell me, couldn't Mrs. Olds swim? She either jumped in the water off the rock she and the other lady had been picnicking on, or else she fell in. It was a terrible thing."

"Aunt Lizzie'd never dive into anything. They have— had—a pool at their place, but I never saw her go near it. She'd wear some kind of a floppy tent out back, but I think she was too self-conscious of what she looked like, you know? If she bared her arm above the elbow in the summer, that was a lot. I'd bet she got into the bathtub dressed like a nun. Wouldn't surprise me a bit. No, she must have fallen in. But what I don't get is how that damned fish got to her so fast. You'd think she could've scrambled out. I didn't think barracuda were that likely to go to the attack, just like that." He snapped his fingers.

"I don't think they are, either. Unless there's blood to attract them."

"Yeah. Probably she cut herself on the rock when she fell in."

"Yeah. Probably. Or on a piece of coral." Or on something. We fell into silence, I in tribute to Mrs. Olds, and her nephew in tribute either to the lady or to the barracuda. "Anyway," I said brightly, and with an infinitude of perception, "here you are! Listen, I thought the plan was for Randy Holland to buy you out, offer you a good bond deal. Let you disentangle yourself from the Olds enterprises."

"It was," he replied wistfully, "and I wish it'd worked out. But after the OPEC people got their act together again and oil prices started back up, Holland sold some of his leases in Texas for a wad of dough and he didn't need me anymore. He shouldn't have been in the oil business anyway, and this way he got out and took his marbles back to television and newspapers, which is what he knows best. So here I am, and I wish I wasn't. Call me the reluctant dragon. And more reluctant than dragon at that."

I clapped him on the shoulder. "It's not so bad. You'll see. Most of these guys are three-quarters bluff. Just hang in there and look like you don't approve. No matter what it is, look like you've got a better idea. That'll get you through."

We separated, and in order to help my employer simmer down I sauntered about to socialize with the big wheels. I talked golf with the lawyer, morality in business with Dorothy Braun, which was, due to the nature of the subject, an extremely brief conversation, and cruise ships with Dolly

Lamoureux. I did not dance with my wife, which made both my wife and Ed Jorgensen very happy.

At eleven Ed closed the bar. "Time, gentlemen," he said, "gentlemen and ladies. We have a big day tomorrow. Got to be ready to plan for the future!" He wouldn't have dared cut off the liquor if Henry Olds had still been alive, which goes to show once again that there's good in everybody. And so to bed.

◻

TWENTY-SIX

◻

Saturday morning and the ritual of the board meeting was under way. Standard etiquette was being observed, I was glad to see, as I got up to discuss the research plans for the coming year; not a creature was stirring, with the exception of those who were disturbed by the deep, regular breathing of their neighbors, breathing which occasionally hovered dangerously at the brink of snoring. Oh, yes, Allie Biedermeier was awake, his expression an amalgam of earnestness, bafflement, and fear, but then Allie Biedermeier was a seconds in board member material.

One reason for my joy at the pervasive somnolence related not to any reluctance to speak in public, but rather to the fact that a year ago in San Sebo I had confidently told the boys that with the dollar way down we were planning on exports to go up. Hence Finch, etc.'s, program for the coming months involved the exploitation of the soon to be booming market for American goods abroad. But despite those prophetic words, the following year produced the worst trade deficit in the nation's history. Nobody listened last year, and nobody would listen this year either as I reversed gear and spoke about the glorious opportunities for advertising from the expected flood of imports that would be landing at the East, West, and Gulf Coast ports over the coming months. Listening simply wasn't manners.

I was thrown off stride by the sudden arousal of the corporate lawyer who had become the newest member of the team. He started taking notes, a shameful breach of etiquette, implying as it did that he intended comparing my predictions for the future with what actually came to pass. Obviously the man was a boor and was unable to appreciate the fact that the purpose of board meetings at places like Pebble Beach is to have board meetings at places like Pebble Beach, and that to want something more of them was unexecutive behavior.

On the other hand, since he was a lawyer, he might only have been preparing a class action suit on behalf of himself and the others in the event that the meeting kept them sitting so long that some among them were afflicted with hemorrhoids. Or fell off their chairs while dozing, thereby suffering grievous bodily harm.

I wondered as I talked if Loretta Holland would accept a commission to feed this guy some doctored rotgut, but in the absence of Henry Olds, neither she nor Dolly Lamoureux had been scooting about dispensing hooch and hangovers. Eventually I got through my fandango and was dismissed. As I walked past the lawyer's chair I took a sidelong glance at his notepaper. He had only been making sketches of what I thought were Japanese yen, German marks, and Spanish doubloons. And dollar signs, both the kind with two vertical strokes such as we use in this country and the single stroke variety favored for some incomprehensible reason by various unAmerican peoples. A right guy, after all. I felt ashamed for having doubted him.

Outside the meeting room wives and camp followers were

assembling for the standard luncheon. Jane, Dolly, and a new female face were chatting it up together, and Loretta was at the bar. As I emerged, I saw her speak to the bartender, who then prepared a clear drink that looked suspiciously like a martini. The lady accepted it, turned around, and approached me.

"Drink, Mr. Franklin?" she asked. "I think this is your usual, isn't it? Vodka martini on the rocks?"

"Yes, it is, but," I said as I looked at my watch, "it's only a little after eleven. I'm too young."

"To drink? Or too young to die?" She favored me with a mocking smile.

"Maybe the truth is somewhere in between," I suggested.

She took the tiniest sip herself. "See?" she said. "It's made with the finest ingredients. Nothing to fret about. I supervised it myself."

When it came to the double entendre Loretta Holland was classier material than I could ever hope to be. "Oh, what the devil," I said. "I give up." I took the drink and hoisted it faceward.

Jane materialized by my side, having made it from the sidelines faster than the speed of light. "Ev, I don't want you drinking that." She turned to Loretta. "It's too early in the day for hitting the bottle," she explained.

"If that's the only reason," Loretta returned, "would you like me to save it for him? Let him have it at noon, say? Before lunch?"

"Under the circumstances," Jane said, "I'd be afraid 'let him have it' might be the operative phrase. No, I think I'll take charge of my husband's martinis. I know what he prefers to have put in them."

"And what he doesn't prefer?" Loretta was actually grinning. For some reason peculiar to herself she was wildly delighted with the insinuation that accepting a drink from her hands would be akin to receiving an already opened bottle of Coke from the loving hands of Lucrezia Borgia.

"You could say that," Jane agreed. "And I will."

The girls stood eyeball to eyeball. I was like a kid whose

nose had been bloodied watching his mother and the mother of his assailant square off at each other for the main event. Loretta gave way first, shifting the dialogue. "Tell me," she urged, "how long has your husband considered himself the sword of the Lord? What does he want from me, or is he bucking for beatification in general? It must be difficult living with him."

"It is," Jane said, "but it'd be more difficult living without him."

I cut in. "Okay. This minuet is getting too rarified for me. Let's sign off, if that's all right with everybody. My wife is right, Mrs. Holland. I shouldn't be drinking now, but thanks for the offer."

"Of course. Perhaps some other time." She walked off and plunged into an overly animated conversation with Dolly Lamoureux, who looked startled that the glamorous Mrs. Holland was acknowledging her existence so fervidly.

"Wow," Jane said.

"Thanks, baby," I said, "but you didn't have to do all that. She wouldn't be doctoring my cocktails. She's nuts, but not that kind of nuts."

"Don't you think I know that?" Jane was annoyed. "What am I, a dummy? It's that smirk on her ladylike face that ticked me off. She was laughing at you, Ev. Who the hell does she think she is, anyway!"

"She doesn't think she's Jesus Christ. That much I know. Maybe Mrs. Christ. She scares me. She doesn't give a damn about a solitary soul except as someone's existence impinges on her comfort and convenience. Look at Kenny. She's supposed to love the guy, but not so much that she hesitates to flush him down to get the heat off herself. And another thing. She finds this poison drink business actually funny! She laughs at it! She laughed when I faced her with Henry Olds's autopsy report. In fact, she roared enough to piss her thousand-dollar jeans. And she was near to hooting right now. I think she enjoyed your coming over to do battle. Why? Why do you think that slays her so much?"

"She plain loves the idea that we're afraid of her. It makes

175

her happy if we think she's some sort of an all-powerful force of nature. An all-powerful harpy is what she is, though, the bitch."

"You think she's laughing because she didn't poison Henry Olds? That she's tickled because we're a couple of misguided dummies?"

"No," Jane said. "I don't think that's it. I mean, who else stood to gain by doctoring old Henry's drinks? She's the only one. She wanted him out of the way as step one in getting control of his company, right? Who else?"

"You're right. Nobody else. Maybe old Dolly, but I don't think so. For one thing she'd never have the balls for it."

After lunch, Jane and I took a drive to get away. My part in the pageant was over, and I decided I'd rather risk Ed Jorgensen's disapproval than dance attendance on the board and their royal consorts. I don't know where we went, but we passed the local airport sign, and on impulse I decided to check in. Holland's pilot had said he'd be out there tuning up the plane and getting it ready for his bosses' departure late on Sunday. But first, I had to confess something to Jane. I had to tell her about the letter I had had trundled down to San Sebo and thence back up to Loretta Holland.

"Oh, Ev," Jane sighed, "you're hopeless. Next time I'll marry Billy instead. He's got more sense."

"Unh unh. Greek lady married her son one time, lad named Rex or Oedipus, something like that. All *sorts* of trouble! You can't imagine!"

There were more sighs. "Okay, okay. What do you hope to gain?"

I told her. I finished by saying, "I'm pretty sure that's why Doc wanted me to have them. There wasn't much he missed on the island, and he must have seen her at it. It's bad enough if Loretta Holland wants to knock off a couple of old turkeys, but when it gets down to her taking aim at me it starts to look serious."

"How about when she goes after me? That look serious too?"

"Well, yes. I suppose it does. You've got a point. You really do."

"Thanks. All right, then, let's go talk to your pilot friend, but for heaven's sake, be careful what you say. After all, if it was deliberate, and if she did it, it means she was prepared to dispense with his services, too. And we don't want a hysterical jock on our hands, do we?"

"Yeah, even if she might have done it to him with sincere regret, unlike with you and me. I'll be careful. My pledge to you."

We found the pilot doodling away at his corporate jet, doing all those manly and sincere things that skilled mechanics can do that make me personally feel so inadequate. "Hi, there," I said cheerily, "how's it going?"

"Not bad, not bad. How's it with you?" He smiled. His eyes wandered, reasonably, off me and onto Jane, and he smiled more broadly.

"Pretty good. This is my wife, Jane. Jane, this is, uh—"

"Jack Bell. Jackie. Anyway, how could I forget, after we went swimming together in that harbor down there. Never forget a good-looking beach date." He laughed.

"Yes," Jane agreed, "and wasn't it fun! You do that often?"

"Nah. Boss sees more than two totalled jets a year on the old expense account, he gets up tight about it. You know how it is with bosses."

"I guess," Jane said. "No sense of fun, bosses. But seriously, do you know what really happened to us? Ev here says it was something with the fuel line. You think they adulterate the gas down there, maybe make a little extra money that way?"

"No way. It's complicated to explain, but aircraft fuel doesn't work like auto's. Nobody's going to get into an underground tank or something, take out gas, pour in water to make a couple of bucks." He shook his head. "Believe me, nobody could've shortchanged us on fuel."

Jane was doing too well so I got jealous and joined the act.

"Yeah, I guess it's not like how you see in the paper when some guy gets ticked off at his ex-wife's new trick so he pours sugar into her gas tank, huh?"

Jack laughed. "Now that's a little different. That could work the same if planes didn't get locked up at night with airport guards and stuff. Once the fuel's in the plane, anybody who knows how and who can get to it can dump sugar in, if they want. I don't know why sugar, it's like a tradition, but damn near anything would do. Sand, if you wanted."

"What would happen?"

"I don't rightly know. Maybe they'd never get off the ground, maybe they'd fly for ten minutes. But sooner or later they sure wouldn't fly no more, that I can tell you."

"Listen, you two," Jane said. "This kind of talk is bad luck. I don't like it. Let's cut it out."

Jack and I exchanged man-smiles: The womenfolk, bless 'em, you know what they're like. "Sure, kid," I said, "We wouldn't want to make the little woman nervous, would we? So who do you like in the World Series, Jack?"

We left ten minutes later. Jane turned to me in the car. "One more little woman line out of you, buster, and I'm going to team up with another little woman with initials Ell Aitch and fry your eggs but good." She settled back and muttered to herself. "Little woman. I'll kill him, so help me."

I sighed. "Looks like none of the girls can keep their hands off me these days. What's a boy to do?"

"Shut up, for starters."

So I shut up. But it was a good day's work for us both, and we knew we were on our way toward bearding the lioness in her platinum-padded den.

TWENTY-SEVEN

The hotel was at the water's edge, and the wind, as it always is in California, was blowing hard and cold. The locals, as they in their turn always are, were in shirt sleeves and even in shorts, pretending that they were warm. The more knowledgeable among the tourists were tucked into sweaters and windbreakers, preferring not to take head colds back east as souvenirs of their stays in sunny California.

Yes, the wind blew relentlessly, and the elegantly twisted trees on the shore, like giant bonsai, stood as living proof of its persistence.

The day was drawing in, though I could still see the fields of wild flowers and weeds and the tree branches dipping and swaying rhythmically to the rise and fall of the gusts. Then, right where she said she would be, I saw Loretta Holland waiting for me. She was leaning back against the rail of a sea wall, silhouetted against a tiny islet a few hundred yards off shore that I knew would be crowded with sea lions, though they were invisible in the half-light. As I drew close, she turned and lifted her face to the wind, seeming to draw life from it, or perhaps defying it, refusing to acknowledge its superior strength. Her hair was tousled and in motion, restless as the growth in the fields. I thought of Medusa.

I had left a message for her, saying I had something urgent to communicate, something from San Scbo from Sarge. I did not append my name to it, but told the phone operator to sign it simply "sugar." When Jane and I got back to the room in the late afternoon, the red message button was flashing. I lifted the phone to inquire, and the operator read me the reply which directed me where and when to meet her before dinner. It was signed "Saccharine." She had still had her cool, but not to the point where she could resist rising to the bait. I was, I estimated, a few points up on the lady.

"I love an evening like this," she said as I drew near. "It's as relaxing as a shower, the wind on your arms, your face, but without the inconvenience of water. I don't like being inconvenienced, Mr. Franklin. Do you?" She put her face into the ocean breeze again and looked as if it were kissing her and she had at last found the lover she could respond to.

"No," I said, "I don't. But speaking as one of the inconveniences you've attempted to eliminate, I doubt that my feelings about it are as fine and sensitive as yours." I wondered vaguely if I should have kept this lonely date. I had told Jane only that I needed to think of what I should do about Loretta Holland, if anything at all, and that I was going for a walk. "I've heard from Sarge, who I gather hasn't heard from you, and he's let me know a little about the way you handle inconveniences, sugar."

She broke off her affair with the elements and turned to face me. Half her face was in the darkness, while the moon brushed a satin glow on her forehead, her cheekbone, her chin. "What do you want, Mr. Franklin, what do you want? And why should I give it to you? I'm not a helpless young thing, you understand, so please be careful. And get to the point." If her flesh was glowing satin, her voice was as acrid as burning plastic.

"Certainly. I'll be happy to. Jane knows I'm out here and she's expecting me back, so let's get to it." I hoped she picked up the point about Jane knowing where I was. She did; she smiled—she sensed I was at least a little bit afraid of her. Score one for the lady.

"That sly old devil Sarge," I went on, "has a couple of sugar bags. He's got this crazy idea that you carted them out to the San Sebo airport and emptied them into the fuel line of the plane. You remember the plane, I'm sure, the one you so generously offered to Mrs. Olds, Jane, and me to carry Mr. Olds's coffin back to the States. At the time I didn't realize exactly how generous you were, that you weren't lending us transportation, but making us a very expensive gift of it on a permanent basis. Too much, Mrs. Holland, really too much."

"Sugar bags don't indicate anything, you know. Judging from the size of his stomach, it's possible friend Sarge has a collection of them, all empty. Even likely, don't you agree? Is that what you dragged me out here for?"

"Correction. I dragged nothing; I invited. You came. See?"

"I stand corrected. I came. I see. And I intend to conquer. Now do *you* see?"

There was a ten second standoff. The night had grown darker, and the moon that had lit the proceedings ducked briefly behind some low-flying scud, fragment of a storm somewhere out in the Pacific. When it reemerged, the light glinted on Loretta's teeth; her lips were parted, possibly in a smile. I decided she had to be in league with the devil; no other explanation was possible.

It was she who broke the silence. "If you think you'll get anywhere producing that half-witted darkie and his terrified minions, you're very much mistaken. And anyway, who in hell are you and what do you think you're up to? I was joking before when I asked if you were bucking for beatification, but now I'm not so sure it's funny. What are you, Mr. Franklin, prosecutor, judge, and jury? What makes you so righteous, so perfect?"

"In as few words as possible, nothing makes me either righteous or perfect. Something makes me sick. And frightens me. You tried to kill three people, four, including the pilot, on an airplane, and I imagine you had nothing against any one of us—with the exception of Elizabeth Olds—and I can't understand why. Or was it that you only wanted to get rid of the Olds woman, because your husband needed to buy her out and she'd said she'd rather die than sell to you? Then when that failed, you murdered her, and I think by now we might as well call it murder and skip the genteel references to getting rid of people. Isn't that right? That's why somebody's got to stop you, and believe me I wish it weren't me. But there's nobody else."

She took out a cigarette, and held the pack toward me. I shook my head. "No, I suppose you wouldn't smoke. No imperfections. I hope you don't hold cigarettes against me too, poisoning the air for the good people?"

"By all means, smoke. The poison is mostly, if not all, yours, and I never judge people for suicide, no matter what you think. But tell me, since you think my pitiful empty sugar bags will never get you in trouble, despite Sarge, despite witnesses, if you had tried to kill Mrs. Olds, wouldn't it have been simpler to have done it on the ground, and without the tiresome complication of those other corpses? And why sugar, of all things, when there's so much sand on the island you could have used?"

"If you want to play 'let's suppose,' first, I wouldn't have had my pail and shovel with me, would I, while there were several bags of sugar so conveniently at hand in the bungalow, in the little kitchenette, sitting there for the asking. And did it ever occur to you that Mrs. Olds was taking her husband's body back, dead as he presumably was of a heart attack, for a second opinion? The silly cow nattered endlessly about new autopsies, about poison, foul play. Murder, then, since you prefer the word. I hate to sound psychoanalytical, but while we're asking questions, does talk of murder lead to sexual arousal with people like you? I have this strange feeling—"

"Actually, no. Unless sexual arousal and nausea are related." I got back to the main event, and could scarcely keep the elation out of my voice. "Then you *did* poison Henry Olds! You doctored his drink with pentobarbitol sodium! I knew it! Is there anything you wouldn't do?"

The laughter started again, too much laughter, the same as the last time I had brought up Henry Olds's death. "I'll take that as two questions. First, there are a few things I wouldn't do, though you haven't touched on any of them yet. But second, and possibly more to the point, I most certainly did not poison that old degenerate, though I do have a certain admiration for the person who did."

"And that was?"

"But my dear Mr. Franklin, you've already told me! It's obvious. I think I'll let you stew about that for yourself. I'm not here in the night air to discuss other people's problems. Get back to me, always a topic of interest. So. Now you accuse me of deciding to destroy a plane and its passengers—"

"And when that failed, you got the pilot out of the way before the results of the investigation were announced. No point in his putting two and two together, was there? It simply isn't your style to have been so concerned with the man's welfare that you'd send him off on a junket. The real Loretta Holland would have fired him for wrecking her plane. You know, that alone, that unprecedented thoughtfulness about someone else, might have tipped me off that something was wrong."

"Thank you," she said wryly. "I'll remember that. It'll never happen again. A temporary aberration."

"At last the truth. I'm sure it won't."

"To continue," she said, "there's only the evidence of a comic imitation Mussolini and some illiterate natives who are so terrified of the man they'd say anything he told them to." She shrugged her shoulders in dismissal. "You'll have to do better. And as for me killing Elizabeth Olds, even if you could establish me at the scene of the crime, the presumed crime, there's little you can add. Suppose we fought. Suppose I jabbed her with her own bloody knitting needle because she pretended to be ignoring me in favor of knitting some hideous rag. Suppose I pushed her off the rock and she was bleeding, and the bleeding attracted that beastly fish. Suppose all that and what have you proved except an accident that frightened me so much that I ran off and said nothing. What have you got, Mr. Franklin, except your own damnable righteousness, to prop up these accusations? Why, you can't even prove I wrote that note, can you? Have you had the handwriting analyzed? Is it mine, or is it Kenny Tillson's? What will that black girl at the hotel say, that creature you're counting on so heavily to bring me to what I'm sure you'll be terming my just desserts? Who gave her the note to deliver? Me?"

"I don't know," I admitted, "what I've got, except a lot of trouble for you. The murders of Mr. and Mrs. Henry Olds, the attempted murders of Mr. and Mrs. Everett Franklin and of Jack Bell. Some evidence, maybe not enough to convict, but enough to tie you up for years, and enough scandal so nobody'll ask you to chair any charity balls until you're old enough to wear your teeth on top of your head instead of a tiara, and think of the money that'll save! We both know you're in this up to your expensive neck, don't we? We both know Kenny didn't tell you about the knitting needle, that you knew because you were right there with your lovely mitts wrapped around it—"

She interrupted. "Yes, all right. Yes, yes, yes. We both know, you and I. I'll give you that. Granted. I had to be there to know about the knitting needle, but now you can grant me something. It'd be my word against Kenny's, if it ever came to that, wouldn't it? My word that he told me, against his word that he never got near that woman and her filthy needle. And while we're at it, you'll get yourself nowhere accusing me of poisoning Henry Olds. You've looked bewildered when I've laughed at you for that, unless bewilderment is nothing more than your normal expression. I've told you I was trained as a nurse. I understand something about drugs. Do you know what pentobarbitol sodium is, Mr. Franklin? Do you have any idea at all about these words you toss about so glibly? I'm sure you don't, so I'll tell you."

She smiled triumphantly, sure of herself, the great beauty

and society leader, queen by natural right, favoring an underling with a friendly word. "Pentobarbitol sodium is commonly prescribed for people who have difficulty sleeping. Do you recall who had difficulty sleeping on San Sebo?" She paused, not for an answer but for dramatic effect. "I see you don't. I'll give you the next clue. This is rather like a television game show, isn't it? I hope you're enjoying it. This should make it easier: the drug is marketed under the trade name Nembutal. Does that ring a bell? Now can you possibly think of the answer?"

My lips started forming the words, but what Loretta Holland had said opened so many doors, so many traps, turned on so many spotlights that I was unable to utter a syllable before she did it for me. She could tell by my expression that a basic truth had penetrated my startled consciousness, and she said, "Precisely. Elizabeth Olds. She had the Nembutal. God knows you should know that, what with your wife popping them into the old bitch's face for three days running. She had the pills that would kill when they were given to someone sodden with alcohol the way her husband was, she had the motive, she had the opportunity, and what's most important, I saw her do it. There you are, little man."

"I don't understand," I stammered. "You can't bluff your way out by hanging this on a dead woman. She had the pills, that's true. And that's all."

"Is it? Her husband was threatening to leave her, for which no one in his right mind could fault the old man. He tortured her the way he tortured the rest of us. He knew perfectly well that acting the great lady was what kept the woman going. But there he was, threatening to kick her off the dunghill she presided over, saying he was going to install that amazon of a model on the throne instead. That's the 'why' of it.

"And," she continued, her smile growing broader, her chin lifted in triumph, "she took him a cup of coffee at the board meeting. She put it down on the service table before she went in, and added cream and sugar. Finally, I'm sure you'll be fascinated to learn, she emptied a capsule of Nembutal—pentobarbitol sodium to you—into the cup, stirred it well, and disappeared to pour it down her loved one's gullet.''

"And you said nothing?"

"Of course not. How was I to know then what it was? He was an old man, and I'm sure she dosed him regularly with a trunkful of medicines. I paid no attention at all to it. Why should I? I had no idea what it was I was seeing. At least not until the old witch began ranting about poisons. Then I started wondering what kind of mischief she was up to." She started the laughter again, her elegant shoulders trembling with delight. "Satisfied? After all, it's you yourself and this pentobarbitol sodium of yours that made me sure of what I suspected."

"But why did you crash that plane if you had nothing to be afraid of from another autopsy?"

"Ah, that's easy. Can't you see it for yourself? Because she had set it up for accusing either the Lamoureux woman or me of murder after the poison was found, and I would have been a much more tempting target, wouldn't I? I was younger, God knows I was better looking, and she had decided I fancied myself as several notches above her, which of course is quite correct. Oh, my, but she must have been surprised and annoyed when that fat black idiot announced that her dear Henry had died of a heart attack. His stupidity nearly spoiled everything for the poor creature. That's why she wanted a second examination, to establish poison as the cause of death. I simply couldn't have used the publicity, Mr. Franklin. As you've said in less polite terms, my charity ball friends wouldn't have been amused. So you see, I had to take action, didn't I?"

"Did you?"

"Yes, I did. I couldn't see any other course."

"We agree about that, at least. You couldn't see any other course. It was more convenient this way, and surely the four of us on the plane ought to have been proud to perish in so worthy a cause."

"There's no need for sarcasm. And if you agree now that

there's nothing you can do but relax and enjoy life, I'm expected back."

"You go ahead, Mrs. Holland. I don't think I want to walk with you. And you'll be hearing much more about this. Or reading about it. We agree on only one thing: There's no need for sarcasm. I apologize. Sarcasm is inadequate for the circumstances. There's a need for much, much more. And I intend to fill that need. Why don't you go?"

I watched her saunter back to the hotel, lit by the moon, a vision of loveliness, at least on the outside. The moon covered her in its light, affectionately, as if aware that at last it had found an object on this earth worthy of being bathed in the softness of its beams. She walked slowly and erect, not a care in the world. What style, what panache, what bravado. I felt sick.

☐
TWENTY-EIGHT
☐

There are, or so I have heard, people who are incurable optimists, people whose faith in themselves or in the Lord or in the ability of man to triumph over adversity is rock solid. I suspect that they are also the people who dote on feature-length cartoons about baby deer and bunny rabbits. I am not one of them, nor is Jane, though we are both what I would consider to be in reasonably good mental health. But we made the mistake of taking the red-eye special from California to New York that Sunday evening, something no one with an urgent problem should consider, no matter what the circumstances.

The red-eye. Board the plane in either San Francisco or Los Angeles at dark and fly all night. Arrive in New York at dawn, in theory ready to face the week, ready for the office or the big meeting, ready to overcome all obstacles and conquer whatever world you may be challenging in your personal life or in your career, be it a matter of backstabbing in the boardroom, monkey business in the bedroom, or, as in our case, murder without consequences.

Baloney. The red-eye would take Pollyanna to the edge of despair and boot the silly twit into outer space. All night sitting up with eyes that sting, beard that itches, feet that grow sticky, back that aches; a night during which it is sometimes possible to doze off briefly into something imitating sleep, but which is actually a state of unconsciousness induced by demons so that they may be free to coat your teeth, tongue, and throat with mouse pelts. The coffee is bitter, the food cardboard, and the poltergeist behind digs its knees into the back of your seat as a reminder that there's no hiding place, even up here.

It is not a time nor is it a place for seeking solutions.

"What's the use?" I asked Jane. "The woman admits she tried to kill us on that plane, but dares us to prove it. And she leaves it open as to whether she quietly watched Lizzie Olds die or could at least have tried to help the woman."

"What she hopes," Jane suggested, "is that you'll think she watched Lizzie Olds being torn apart and that knowing you can't do anything about it will drive you bananas."

"And then the business with Henry Olds. What can we believe? Who poisoned the man? His wife or Loretta Holland? I'm inclined to believe her on that one. Lizzie killed her husband to keep him from ditching her, which is why Loretta finds it too, too amusing that I should have accused her."

"I'm sure you're right. She takes it as a compliment, you thinking she could have done it. She enjoys that. It shows you're afraid of her, which to Loretta Holland means that you respect her."

The stewardess put a container of coffee in front of me. I knew it would taste like pencil shavings, but I sipped it anyway in the hope that some coffee flavor would come through. It didn't, though the pencil flavor was much enhanced by a delicate touch of liquid mulch. In some gloomy way I drew satisfaction from the experience; I would have been disappointed if anything pleasant had transpired on the red-eye.

I turned sideways and pushed my cheek into the chairback, trying to grab a microscopic slice of sleep. As I closed my eyes I heard Jane, with equal despair, say, "Maybe she's right. Maybe you've got no cause to take this on yourself. What business is it of yours?"

We passed the rest of the trip in silence, except that in my head Jane kept asking what business it was of mine, and Loretta kept repeating her query as to whether or not I was bucking for beatification.

Over the next weeks and months I asked myself the same questions and found I was unable to answer. Was I being propelled by personal motives? Why did I lack an equal contempt for Lizzie Olds, who was just as much a murderer as Loretta Holland? Why did I instead feel sick and sorry about pompous, unattractive Lizzie, and reserve my moralizing for the lovely Loretta?

I've noticed over the years, though I've never known it to be mentioned by psychologists, not even in the science edition of *The New York Times,* that boredom is the great healer; kick an insoluble problem around long enough to drive yourself batty, and if you're anywhere near being otherwise emotionally stable you'll finish by becoming so tired of it that the mind will grow numb, the memory will fade, and finally, the unbearable mess will slip from view. What psychiatrists should say to their patients isn't that they should look for solutions, but something like, "Forget it, pal. You'll feel better."

Personally, I forgot it, except sometimes late at night. And I felt better—except sometimes late at night. But there was someone else who decided not to forget, someone I had overlooked. I had forgotten that deep within that brittle facade, below the fountain of merry bitchery, Kenny Tillson had been badly hurt. All of us have some treasured memory of a friend from what we rightly or wrongly think were the golden days, the days of happiness and love and innocence, the time when we were young and beautiful—or at least we manage to kid ourselves into reshaping the past that way. By her calculated deceit, by her tossing Kenny to the wolves so casually, Loretta Holland, née Saunders, had pushed her dirty hand back into Kenny's happy youth and smudged it. And he couldn't forget that.

How does a guy like Kenny handle a situation like that? By turning it into a joke with a sprinkling of malice and a dab of dirt for spice. He talked Loretta up in the world he inhabited, the land of television and glamor personalities, and as if the truth weren't juicy enough, the stories grew ever more exotic. There was a lava flow of gossip—hot, dirty, and with the added thrill of danger. Someone with money and influence became interested, and somehow down in San Sebo obtained a copy of the autopsy report on Henry Olds. Just for kicks, I'd guess. It's likely friend Sarge emerged with enough cash to purchase a new wardrobe of unwashed T-shirts. The report was published in one of the weekly sheets for the glamor-starved that are on display at supermarket checkouts. The Hollands were named. A beautiful model whose name was now Charlotta was quoted on her version of Henry Olds's vindictive stance vis-à-vis Randolph Holland's financial troubles.

Charlotta got a movie contract.

More stories, replete with a thousand repetitions of the sacred word "alleged," the talisman that wards off libel suits—stories about Lizzie Olds and the mysterious note that removed Dolly Lamoureux from the scene of the crime, surfaced and found their ways into print. Dolly was interviewed, her hair newly and most unattractively sculpted for the edification and entertainment of the television audience. Scientific articles about the care and feeding of barracuda could be observed.

Loretta Holland's name appeared less often on the society pages, and more frequently in the weeklies. One headline asked, "Did she fall or was she pushed?" Another story claimed that Loretta was being considered for the female lead in a major TV series as the beautiful and wealthy villainess around whom the plot revolved. That item asked, "Will she act or will she be herself?"

Ironically, nothing appeared about the plane crash, the only crime I knew with absolute certainty could be attributed to the lady, the only one to which she had cheerfully confessed. An almost young assistant district attorney in the New York district, the type whose wild eyes and set lips are a nightly feature on the evening news as he grabs at whatever publicity might further his political ambitions, made an announcement: He would investigate the likelihood that a prominent local citizen had been involved in the deaths of several other prominent citizens. The fact that the putative crimes had been committed far from his jurisdiction was pushed aside. The key word was "prominent." In prominence lies media exposure and political advancement. It came to nothing, but it achieved its purpose; the man's media coverage graduated from the local news and went national; there's good in everything, if not everybody.

Loretta Holland became last year's national treasure. Not even déclassé entertainers, a species she would have totally avoided in the past, were on hand as escorts. If I had thought harder about Loretta's attitude toward inconveniences, even when she herself was the inconvenience, I might have anticipated what ensued.

> Somerville, NJ, May 14. A single-engine plane piloted by Loretta Holland, wife of media magnate Randolph Holland, crashed today five miles off the Jersey shore near Asbury Park. As far as can be determined as of this time, the plane had run out of fuel in mid-flight. An airport attendant reports that the plane was fueled to full capacity before takeoff. "There must have been a leak in the line," he surmises, "but Mrs. Holland should have seen the reading on the gauge. She was an experienced pilot." A private service will be held. . . .

There was no point in grieving over the loss of life. I was sure Loretta wouldn't have, not even when it was her own. Something was missing in the woman: When life was good it was to be lived; when it went sour, why bother keeping it around? Loretta was in Loretta's way, just as Elizabeth Olds had been, just as Jane and I and the pilot had been, and obstructions are moved aside, aren't they? It's only sensible. I could regret the loss of life, but not the loss of Loretta Holland, and in some peculiar way they were two different things, life and Loretta, which was, I expect, what made the woman so terrifying. I knew she'd be resting in peace, because she had done what she wanted to do, right up to the end, and had nothing to regret.

There is, I suddenly realized, something good about getting back to work. No, I don't mean that it helps the healing process by using up energy, or that it eases a return to the normal world. I mean only that it diverts attention from anything that matters very much, and offers problems to noodle over that might even be amenable to solution, thus proving their supreme unimportance.

In my case, the morning mail in the office had regurgitated a missive from Buford Butz, known in the advertising industry as Superputz, a man who blighted by his presence as marketing director a medium size newspaper in southern Mississippi for which Finch, etc., was the advertising agency. Buford, or Binkie, as we called him, though only to his face, had commissioned a survey of the readers of his morning edition. There were some puzzling results he wanted my advice about.

Print media like to show advertisers that readership is much greater than circulation alone would indicate; people pass along the paper or the magazine to others. In Binkie's case, there were 2.3 adults in each household that got a home-delivered morning paper. But the survey showed 3.3 adult readers of every copy. Were intruders pushing through the windows so they could set themselves down for a good read? Sounds great, huh? Lotsa readers! But wait: The average income per reader was lower than it should have been for this prosperous little city. That's not great. Advertisers aren't interested in reaching people without money.

Binkie's letter to me asked, "Do you suppose that the colored girls, instead of cleaning the house, are goofing off to read the paper? Maybe that could be what's pulling readership up and pushing income down? What do you think, old buddy?"

"Dear Binkie," I wrote back, "smart thinking. And maybe the colored girls" (I winced; give me a *little* credit) "are even taking the paper home to their families, which would pull the income level of readers down even further. You might look into some kind of program to encourage the lady of the house to keep her paper away from the girl, like a home economics column on keeping fish fresh by wrapping it in newsprint. Incidentally, we both know of course that the one advantage of newspapers that television can never take away, is that you can't wrap a fish in a TV set. Well, old buddy yourself, I'm sorry to have to tell you that those other colored folk over there in Japan have been test marketing a TV set that's fish-wrappable. They've been placing them on those boats off the Pacific Coast, the ones that have been poaching on all our good American tuna fish—"

I did indeed write that letter. I won't, however, pretend I sent it, except to Jane. It made me feel better. It's the little things in life that count. I might even go back to San Sebo some day, though only to hide dead fish inside Sarge's desk, or, if they're minnow-size, to drop them down his ample cleavage, though that might constitute cruel and unusual punishment—to the fish.

Did I say? Randolph Holland got married again. To a younger edition of what looked like, from her pictures at those charity balls, a younger edition of the same tomato. All's well that ends, I guess, so long as it does.